THE DARK TRAIL

After the rest of her family were killed by Indians, ten-year-old Clara Somers was enslaved by them. Ten years later, she escaped, intending to inform General Sheridan of Sitting Bull's plans to annihilate all whites west of the Mississippi. Todd Bonner, a rancher, offered to take her to Sheridan, but nothing went according to plan and death was at hand. Then, too, there was the renegade Cheyenne warrior, Cold Star, who was determined to take Clara — or die in the attempt.

Books by Paul K. McAfee
in the Linford Western Library:

BONNER

PAUL K. McAFEE

THE DARK TRAIL

Complete and Unabridged

LINFORD
Leicester

First published in Great Britain in 1996 by
Robert Hale Limited
London

First Linford Edition
published 1998
by arrangement with
Robert Hale Limited
London

British Library CIP Data

McAfee, Paul K.
    The dark trail.—Large print ed.—
    Linford western library
    1. Western stories
    2. Large type books
    I. Title
    823.9'14 [F]

    ISBN 0-7089-5279-8

Published by
F. A. Thorpe (Publishing) Ltd.
Anstey, Leicestershire

Set by Words & Graphics Ltd.
Anstey, Leicestershire
Printed and bound in Great Britain by
T. J. International Ltd., Padstow, Cornwall

This book is printed on acid-free paper

This book is dedicated with
love and appreciation to those
companions of my youth, Aldena,
Loran, Fern and Wilma

1

THE wagon moved across the high plains, its white canvas cover gleaming in the hot sun. The land was deceptive, seeming level from the distance, but proving rough and rocky, uneven and rolling. Grass swept the bellies of the huge, lumbering oxen and swished about the tall wheels of the wagon. Insects darted and buzzed about the head of the man driving the oxen. On the high seat, the ten-year-old girl watched the world about her, seeing little but an ever retreating horizon, an ever-burning sun and the rumps of the slow, patient animals pulling the huge wagon.

Walter Somers had left Vincennes, Indiana, six months ago with his wife, a small son of three years, his daughter, Clara, and all his worldly goods. With these he struck out for the West,

seeking new lands and home.

"Dade Jenkins," he told his wife, "writ me that in Wyomin' there's land as rich as gold an' you kin sign on a hundred an' sixty acres, on water, an' graze as much as you need around your plot."

Lilly Somers was a quiet, seldom-spoken woman. She followed her man in whatever he did. Leaving home and family, the farm that had just started to produce well, she still did not hesitate. She followed her knowledge of Biblical instruction from her youth: her husband was the man of the house and she would do as he wished, keep the home, cook the meals, sew the clothes to wear and bear the children. Beyond that her horizons did not reach.

She rode in the back of the wagon or walked. Little Henry, three years old, played in the wagon, now and then rode the wide back of the gentlest oxen, and walked with his father, stretching his small legs to fit the striding of the man he adored.

So the days passed and months and now Laramie was near, or so the crude map Dade Jenkins had drawn him indicated. Somers judged it to be at least another week, and they would be there, find their spring or creek, their source of water, and stake their claim. His mild blue eyes searched the horizon and saw the nubs of mountains appearing, low and small, above the heat-wavering line.

"Them's the tips of mountains," he called to the daughter, Clara, riding on the wagon seat. "They look awful small frum here, but child, when we get closer, they will reach almost to the heavens."

"How soon, Papa?" she asked. "How soon will we be there?"

"In about another four or five days," he said. "We'll travel easier now, rest more often and make it to the fort in good time."

"Papa, are there Indians out here?" she asked, her voice small in the immensity of the world about her. It

3

was mid-afternoon. They had stopped by a buffalo wallow where some aspens had sprung up from a small spring on the lip of the wallow. There he had watered the animals, let them graze an hour while the family ate a meagre lunch in the shade of the trees.

"I wuz told this is Cheyenne country. There may be some of them about, but maybe not. A scout in St Joe told me there were Shoshoni in this area and some Ute. We've been lucky since we left the wagon train and decided to cut over to Fort Laramie. I think we are safe now, this close to the soldiers."

"What's the difference between those two tribes you just said about?" she asked.

He shrugged, slapping at a huge fly that poised on the hip of the nearest oxen. "I don't rightly know, honey. The Cheyenne are horse Indians. They ride wild ponies and hunt deer and buffalo while riding rickety-split alongside them. Or so I've been told."

4

Clara laughed, her voice a silver tinkle in the hot air of the plains. Lilly Somers pushed her shoulders through the canvas and wiped sweat from her face. "What little air there is up here feels good," she said. "It's like an oven in the wagon. But little Harry's asleep. Scoot over, honey, I'll join you."

She settled on the seat and spoke to her husband. "Then we don't have to worry about Indians?" she asked, having heard the last part of her husband's conversation with Clara.

"Well, I won't say we are absolutely safe from them now, but being this close to the fort helps. We'll still be careful and watch for them."

The Somers' wagon was a full day out of Fort Laramie. It was after four in the afternoon when they came upon a small copse of silver aspens. A small stream wandered out of the midst of the trees, and wound away into the plain. Walter could see that it was a favorite watering place for animals.

Hoof prints of various kinds were in evidence.

"We'll camp here tonight," he said. "We're about a day's travel from the fort. We can bathe and have a good supper and a full breakfast and be in the fort by sundown tomorrow."

Lilly sighed. "That sounds wonderful," she said. "To be able to bathe freely will be a boon."

He drew the wagon into a small glade beside the stream and busied himself unhitching the oxen and taking them to a stand of high grass nearby. With the lushness of the graze, he was not worried they would wander.

Clara and her mother, with towels and a bar of soap disappeared further into the trees, and he heard their voices, and Clara's silvery laughter as they enjoyed the first real bath they had had for months. Little Harry stayed with him, his eyes big and round as he followed his father's footsteps and got in the way, as Walter prepared a fire for their evening meal.

It was a clear night. A small breeze found its way over and through the aspens, cooling the campsite. They ate their meal as the sun sank in red and orange skies. High clouds caught the colors and reflected them into the purple dusk as the shadows crept over the plains.

The family having eaten the meal, Lilly read from the Bible for a while and then from a small book of poetry, Harry with his head in her lap, and Clara listening, lying on a blanket and watching the stars appear. Walter gazed into the fire, musing, thinking of the day ahead. A new life was so near.

They went to bed, Walter and Lilly, with little Harry, in the wagon. Clara rolled in blankets and a ground sheet beneath the wagon. The family dog slept beside her, his back against her side. She watched the fire die, the coals grow dark and then she slept.

★ ★ ★

They came with the dawn! There was a dozen of them, young Cheyenne warriors, returning home from a foraging trip against the Utes. They had watched the wagon the entire day and watched the whites during the evening meal and the hour or so following, until they settled for the night.

The dog sprang from Clara's side, barking, and was speared by a young warrior leaning from his rushing pony. Walter leaped from the wagon, cocking his rifle, and firing into the treetops as arrows darted through him front to back. He stiffened, cried out and fell, quivering as life left his body.

Lilly crouched in the wagon bed, screamed as warriors clambered through into the body, from the front and back, and threw herself across the wailing child, Harry. One of the warriors seized her by the hair and, jerking her head up, slashed her throat with his knife. The other seized the child and tossed him out of the wagon. The infant struck his head against a protruding

rock and died instantly.

The wild yipping, the screams of the warriors, the turmoil of the moment, struck Clara dumb. She crouched, shivering, back of a wagon wheel, and watched as several of the warriors surrounded the oxen, and shouting and laughing, slaughtered the huge 'whoa-haws' one by one.

The things within the wagon were tossed out and rummaged through. Some of Lilly's dresses were draped about the bronzed, naked shoulders of warriors. One turned a corset this way and that, puzzled at what he had, and finally gave up with a grunt and tossed it away.

Clara watched and wept silently. She squatted as close to the ground as she could, sheltered partially by the wagon wheel. Then she saw a warrior approaching. He came close and stood beside the wheel, looking down at her. He was tall and sweating, his rancid odor coming to her nostrils. Slowly he knelt and peered through the spokes of

the wheel at her, his obsidian pupils gleaming.

Suddenly, quick as a striking viper, his bronze hand darted through the wheel-spokes and seized her wrist. She screamed for the first time, shrill and piercing. She struggled as he grunted and sprawled beneath the wagon, grasping her with both hands.

He pulled her, kicking and screeching, from beneath the wagon and rose, shaking her viciously, making her head bounce back and forth against his chest. The violent abuse caused her to cease her screeching and pause to catch her breath.

A painted warrior left the slaughter of the oxen and dashed up before the one holding Clara, a wide grin on his face.

"Toss her into the air, Eagle Feather," he yelled. "I will catch her on my lance and send her to wherever the white-eyes go when the spirit leaves them."

Eagle Feather shook his head. "No, Spotted Elk, she is mine. I shall take

her to my father's lodge."

"Why? Your father needs no slaves. He has had two wives and two daughters."

"My mother has been ill for all the cold moons, and is still sick in her lungs. She needs help in the lodge and can train this one to do her work. The rest can do the other work."

"Well, she is your problem, not ours," Spotted Elk grunted. The warriors gathered around Eagle Feather. They talked quickly and showed what they had gathered up: Somers' rifle, some shot and powder from the wagon, Lilly's jewelry, what there was of it, and selected pieces of her clothing for squaws of individual warriors.

"We will go," ordered Eagle Feather, who was the leader. "Soldiers of the white-man's fort might be coming out to meet this wagon. The girl will ride with me." Spotted Elk had explained to the others that Eagle Feather was taking Clara to become a slave to his mother.

11

One of the warriors brought the leader's pony to him. With a single bound, he mounted and, reaching down, grasped Clara by the arm and lifted her on to the mount before him. He said something to her in his language. His voice was soft and his eyes were no longer piercing, but held a gentle light. Reaching down she grasped the pony's mane and the Indian's arm reached around her for support.

With wild yips, yells and whoops, the warriors left the scene of violence. They rushed up the gentle prairie slope away from the spring and small copse of trees, and in a moment were away from the wagon and the dead and dying oxen.

A little breeze reached tenuous fingers into the campsite, stirring the leaves of the aspens and lifting the ripped and tattered cover of the now overturned wagon. On the ground lay Lilly's Bible. The breeze riffled the pages and passed on to touch the blood-smeared hair of little Harry's

head. The last oxen strained, quivered and died with a low, mournful grunt and silence lay over the campsite.

Clara Somers was whisked away from her life as she had known it up to now, racing away from fearsome scenes which would haunt her for the rest of her life. Held tightly against the body of the leader of the Cheyenne warriors, she shut her eyes and struggled against tears. The racing of the pony pounded at her small body. She lapsed into a dull stupor, no longer feeling grief or fear. She just was.

May 16, 1866, near Fort Laramie, Wyoming, Clara Somers entered a new and frightening world. She was ten years old.

★ ★ ★

Clara Somers stood looking down into the black, squinted eyes of the Cheyenne woman. The woman was Eagle Feather's mother, old and

wrinkled. They were in the lodge of Eagle Feather's parents. His father was meeting with the council discussing the stirring message the tribe had received the day the young warriors arrived back from their dashing foray against the whites.

The old woman spoke to her in Cheyenne tongue, which Clara, of course, did not understand. Clara was weak with fright, and was hungry from having received little food on the trip to the Indian encampment. She was fatigued from the rough trip on horseback, held tight by the warrior so she would not fall.

The old woman's keen eyes saw all this. She turned her head and spoke softly to one of the younger women in the lodge. "Take her to the bathing place and see that she is clean. Then dress her in clothes proper for our lodge. After that we will feed her."

"What is to become of her?" asked the young woman addressed as she

came forward. "Is she to be put to death?"

The old mother shook her head. "No. She is to live in our lodge and will be my hands and feet now that I can not breathe good and it wearies me to work the fields and do the skins."

The young woman took Clara by the hand. Clara's eyes widened and she jerked away. The old woman shook her head and said to Clara, "Do not be afraid, little one. No harm will come to you in this lodge."

Not knowing the language, somehow the tone of the old woman's voice, a slight smile in the eyes, a gentleness of expression, told her she was safe. She allowed the daughter to lead her from the lodge.

In a few days Clara began to learn the language. Words conveyed their meaning, single utterances became sentences, and in a short time the intelligent young child was able to converse with her captors.

Past life dimmed. The horror of her parents' and brother's death softened and became a dream, recalled now and then. Eagle Feather talked to her daily and the old woman looked upon her as another daughter. The father of the lodge, One-Who-Leaps-Highest, accepted her stoically, but was kind. In a short while Clara Somers, dressed in deerskins and small pelts, the laced sandals of the women, looked like any other ten- or twelve-year-old Indian maid, doing her work in the lodge, going about her day as a child of an Indian tribe.

One thing eventually brought attention to this auburn-haired, pale-skinned child. She could run. In games where running was part, she excelled. Finally, in a contest with some boys of the tribe, distances marked and refereed by men, she outran them, reaching the marks far ahead of her nearest opponent, to the chagrin of the boys.

Because of this, she was given her tribal name, Girl-With-Feet-Of-Deer.

Later it was shortened to Fleet-Foot, and secretly she named herself Clara Fleetfoot. Clara Somers was a child and then a young woman in the lodges of the Cheyenne.

2

AL ROONEY came to the doorway of the office and, leaning against the doorframe, looked at Clint Steele, where he was working on the ranch books. Clint looked up, and put down his pencil.

"Something on your mind, Al?" he asked. He leaned back and rolled a cigarette, lighting it and drawing in a deep breath.

"You got some company out here, boss," the older man said. "D'you know a mountain man by the name of Homer Bell?"

Clint frowned, thinking, then shook his head. "Nope, can't recall that I do. Is that who is wantin' to talk to me?"

Al nodded. "Him an' a young woman," he said.

Clint brought himself forward and looked at Rooney. "A young woman?

18

Ummm, maybe you'd better bring them in, so I can get a good look at both of them."

Al left the doorway and returned a moment later, stepping aside to let the huge, hulking bulk of a man through the doorway, followed by a slender young woman dressed in deerskin.

"You the boss of this outfit?" the man asked, his voice rumbling deep and low from a giant chest, sounding like thunder rolling from a barrel. His eyes, sharp blue and cold as ice, glinted from beneath dark brows, the same color as his hair which hung below his coat collar, long and greasy. His beard, flecked with white, reached halfway down his chest. On his head was a cap of beaver, rarely seen now, since beaver had been killed out of this part of Wyoming.

Clint nodded. "I'm the owner of this spread. What can I do for you and" — he nodded and smiled at the woman — "for the young lady?"

"My name is Clara . . . Somers."

He noticed that her English was rather halting, and her words pronounced as though she was unsure of the language.

"I'm Clint Steele." Clint called to Al. "Have Emmy bring us some coffee and some of those donuts we had for supper." He turned back to his visitors.

"I'm Homer Bell," the big man said. "Me and this young lady would like to talk to you about something that you may or may not believe. The marshal in that little town, Red Bluff, said you was a pretty sensible feller, and might listen to us."

Clint smiled. "You are welcome here, and I'll listen. About me being sensible, there might be some who would disagree."

Emmy Steele entered with a tray holding cups and a pot of coffee and a plate of donuts. She smiled as she set the tray on the desk.

"This is my wife, Emmy," Clint introduced her. "Emmy, why don't you draw up a chair and join us . . . you

too, Al." He gestured to a chair by the door.

"This is Al Rooney, folks. He is my *segundo*. In fact, he runs the place."

The big man looked intently at Rooney. "Seems I have heard about you, Rooney. Somethin' about bein' a fast gun."

Al simply met his gaze with a steady stare. "Man hears all sorts of things," he said softly. Bell nodded and turned his attention back to Clint.

"Miss Somers here has a story to tell you. I think it's facts, what she has to say. Others might disagree with me. But I'm gonna let her talk and then we'll see what comes frum it."

Clint eyed him silently for a long moment. "From your outfit I'd guess you are one of the few left of the mountain men," he said. "Don't see many of your kind, not around here anyway."

Bell shrugged. "Times change. The huntin' an' trappin' is about all done in these mountains. Maybe up around

the Wind River country, or around the Yellerstone, thar's some animals left. But that's another story. Let the lady tell hers first."

Clint nodded. He looked at the young woman. About twenty or so, I'd judge, he thought. Been with the Indians, maybe an escaped captive. Clara took his nod and his look as signal for her to begin.

"My family was killed by Cheyennes ten years ago. We were on our way to Fort Laramie. My father had judged we were a day or so away from the fort when it happened. He, my mother, and a baby brother were all killed. It just so happened that the leader of the party had a mother ill and he saved me for a slave to do her work. I was taken into their lodge and grew up with them. The mother was elderly and ill and died after I was captured. For the next years I lived in the lodge and was finally adopted by the father, who was a minor chief, as a daughter."

Emmy had tears in her eyes. "You

poor thing," she murmured. "To have to endure such a life, after seeing your parents and brother murdered by members of the tribe."

The young woman shrugged. Her skin was tanned dark, making her near the coloration of an Indian. Her hair was braided and hung down over both shoulders, long and dark auburn, reaching to her breasts. Her dress of soft deerskin, the band about her head, and the moccasins, strong and stitched in designs, made her appear to be an Indian squaw.

"It was a rough life, compared to what I remembered from my living in Indiana. But as time went on, and it was understood by the tribe that I was slave only to the family of One-Who-Leaps-Highest, I was not teased, nor was I tortured in any manner. Then when Red Leaf, that was the old mother, died and I was adopted by her husband as a daughter, I became part of the tribe and there was no question about my status."

She fell silent, hesitated, and then continued, "That is enough of why I was with the Cheyenne. Being able to move around and not be noticed, I realized an important council was being held and managed to get close enough to listen. Mr Bell showed up in camp about that time, and I told him what I had heard."

Clint looked at the huge mountain man. "How did you manage to get this woman away from the Cheyenne?" he asked. "And I think there must be something mightily important for you to risk your life, and hers, to bring her out."

Bell nodded. "I have known old One-Who-Leaps-Highest for a long time. Did him a favor one time, an' he's been pretty friendly ever since. Whenever I'm in his territory I make a visit just to make shore he's still friendly. This time I saw this woman and knowed right away she wuzzn't Injun. No white woman kin walk like an Injun woman, no matter

how hard they try. Jist somethin' about their build, I guess."

Clara Somers sat quiet, her body, her eyes still, her face emotionless. She does a pretty good job of acting like an Indian woman, Emmy thought. She doesn't make a move, hardly breathes when she's not talking.

Clint offered the makings of a cigarette to Bell. He declined and fell silent.

"So here you are, however you managed to get away from the Cheyenne," he said. "Just what is so important?"

Clara Somers raised her eyes and looked at him intently. "The Indians are all going to come together at one place and make war upon the white people, ranchers, the army, towns — all of them."

"That is not new thinking," Clint said softly. "There has been such rumors ever since Lewis and Clark made their first explorations through the West."

"There's more. Sitting Bull, the Sioux chief, has sent word for all Cheyenne and Sioux to come together at a place in the Dakotas near a river called Little Big Horn. There they will challenge the whites, wipe out their army and begin to destroy all ranches and homes, until all Indian lands are free of the white-eyes."

Clint was silent. He had fought through the Civil War, and had for a short time been assigned to General Philip Sheridan who, by orders of President Grant, was in charge of all forces west of the Mississippi River. Sheridan had further orders from President Grant to contain the Indian problem that was plaguing the western areas. But, being on staff work, Clint had not experienced any of the Indian wars that had taken place immediately following the Civil War.

Upon discharge, he and a friend had decided to go into horse ranching, and had come to Red Bluff, Wyoming, where he had inherited a holding called

Red Bluff Basin. Here his ranch lay upon 60,000 acres of choice grazing, and his efforts to create an outstanding horse-breeding venture was progressing. But in all this time, he had had no trouble with the Indians of that locality.

He looked at Clara. "Why do you come to me? I have no idea what it is you want from me?"

Bell stirred and his deep voice rumbled as he spoke. "She wants to get a personal message to General Sheridan. About the gatherin' together of so many Injuns. We was told you might be able to escort her to him, since you knowed him once."

Clint wondered how Bell and the woman had come upon the knowledge that he had known General Sheridan. He let that go for the moment and asked the one question that had run through his mind during the entire discussion.

"Indians tend to fight and then run. They do not have the concept of staying with a battle until the last man

is dead. So Sitting Bull can't expect any huge number of tribes to reach across ethnic lines and fight under his leadership until all the whites are killed off. How many does he expect to gather up and put against the United States armed forces this side of the Mississippi?"

Clara was silent a moment and then said softly, "The number I heard mention would be equal to twelve thousand warriors!"

Clint stared at her and his skin crawled! He felt the hair on his arms rise and a chill reached deep within him. *12,000 Cheyenne and Sioux warriors in one place?*

He looked at Emmy and saw her lips trembling, her face pale. Al Rooney grunted and shook his head. A long silence spread itself about the room.

★ ★ ★

Cold Star was furious! He had asked One-Who-Leaps-Highest for the white

woman. He could not marry her, but she would be his first concubine. But the old sub-chief had merely grunted that the woman was a slave and unworthy to live in the lodge of such an important warrior as Cold Star. Girl-With-Feet-Of-Deer was at that time doing all the work of the seriously ill Red Leaf, the mother of the lodge.

Then, when the old woman died, Cold Star again approached the sub-chief for Girl-With-Feet-Of-Deer, and again was refused. In a council soon after Cold Star's second offer for the slave girl, One-Who-Leaps-Highest announced that the girl was now to become his daughter. Cold Star was angered. He knew that the purchase price of the girl would now be much more than when she was a slave. He made no more offers for her, but his anger toward the girl and toward the old sub-chief smouldered through the years.

Now she was gone! Sometime during

the week of the big council gathering in his camp she had slipped away. He was advised that probably she had been attacked by a cougar, killed and carried away. Or she had wandered away and fallen, broken a leg and died of thirst and starvation.

This Cold Star questioned. The mountain man, called Bell, had been in the camp at the time and had left during the dark of the night, the same time the girl apparently wandered away from the confines of the huge camp.

Cold Star reasoned that the white man had enticed the girl to go with him, or had kidnapped and carried her away. Unless . . . the girl had heard the council talk that Sitting Bull of the Sioux was calling for all Cheyenne tribes to meet with the Sioux and wipe out the white-eyes once for all.

If this was true, then she must be stopped before she could take the plan to the leaders of the white-eyes, and in particular, to the blue-coats and Buffalo Soldiers who skirmished back

and forth with the Indians of the plains.

This in mind, Cold Star left the encampment and, huge as it was, began a search around the circumference. It took a long time, cutting back and forth, working farther and farther away from the camp. Two days after he began his search, he struck their trail.

The white man, Bell, Cold Star admitted to himself, was very good at hiding sign. But the Indian located tracks that could only be his and that of the woman. He followed for a half-day, and then turned back to the camp.

There he related to the Cheyenne chief what he had found. The chief called in One-Who-Leaps-Highest and questioned him. The old man had no answers. He was chastened and lost influence among his people. The woman he had made his daughter had turned against them! Cold Star and the chief knew there was more than that involved.

She perhaps carried a secret that

could very well spell disaster to the plans of Sitting Bull, if she was allowed to tell it to the white-eyes and soldier chiefs.

"Find her," the chief told Cold Star. "Find her and bring her back for punishment. If that is not possible, kill her before she can disclose the plans she heard."

Cold Star left the camp, prepared for a long journey: one that could end only one way, capture or death of Clara Somers, Girl-With-Feet-Of-Deer.

3

CLINT STEELE, accompanied by Todd Bonner, dismounted before the corrals and turned their horses over to a wrangler to be unsaddled and cared for.

"Come on in, Todd." Clint dusted trail dust off his shoulders and nodded to his companion. "There's hot coffee I suspect and then we'll let you talk to Bell and Miss Somers."

Al Rooney came from the bunkhouse and joined them. Rooney was a slender man in his late forties. He was taciturn, his light-blue eyes cool and clear. He wore a .44 calibre six-gun on his right hip, the butt worn and serviceable. He nodded to Bonner.

"Howdy, Todd, good to see you again." He looked at Clint. "Did yore old army boss reply to yore telegram?" he asked.

Clint nodded soberly. "Yes. Come on in with us. I'll make them acquainted with Todd, and tell them what we have learned."

"Bell's in the cookshack. I'll get him and join you," Al said. Todd and Clint proceeded into the house, met at the door by Emmy Steele. She led them into the kitchen, and with them grouped about the table, served coffee.

Clara Somers appeared at the doorway and the men stood, while Clint introduced her to Bonner. "Mr Bonner is from the Dakotas," he explained. "He is, or was, a US marshal in search of a criminal. Now, he is ready to return, but has decided to buy some of my horses and ship them to his ranch."

Bonner shook hands with her and Clint brought her a chair. Al Rooney and Homer Bell arrived as she was being seated and joined the group about the table. Emmy busied herself with more coffee and some fresh biscuits

and a pot of honey.

"Did you get a telegram off to Sheridan?" Bell asked, his big hands busy buttering a biscuit and applying a generous glob of honey on its center.

Todd nodded. "He wired back that there wasn't that many Cheyenne in the West that would get together just because Sitting Bull suggested it. He didn't believe the number."

Clara's face showed her astonishment. "Does he know how many small tribes, related to Sioux and Cheyenne, there are who will jump at the chance to make war on the whites?"

"He knows what his scouts and spies have told him, and what Indian agents have reported," Clint said. "It's very difficult to get a true count of just what the Cheyenne and Sioux population is."

Clint continued and looked at Clara, "He suggests that you come to Fort Abraham Lincoln, at Bismark, and report to him there. That's in the Dakota Territory."

"A long way from here," Clara murmured.

"That is why I had Todd come along to talk to you. He is on his way back to his ranch in Dakota Territory. He has agreed to escort you to Bismark, if you desire to go."

Bonner nodded. "We can take the rails to Lincoln, Nebraska, and stages north from there. Otherwise it would be a hard trip from here to Bismark over country."

"An' the Sioux reservation is between you an' Bismark if you went across country frum here," the mountain man said. "You'd have to go around it, fer it'd be too dangerous to try to slip through now, with Sittin' Bull gettin' th' Injuns all stirred up."

Clara sipped her coffee and looked down at the table, thinking. She was certain Cold Star would attempt to find her, once her absence was known. The train and the stages would be faster, taking her away from this area quickly. And certainly the Indian could not

travel as fast as the train. She raised her head and looked at Bonner.

"If General Sheridan won't take our word for this uprising, and the number of warriors involved, why would he trust my word face to face?"

Bonner shrugged. "Sometimes hearing it from the lips of those who were there makes a greater impact. Phil Sheridan is no dummy. He knows he's sitting on a powder keg, what with Sitting Bull stirring the Indians up." He looked at Homer Bell. "Crazy Horse is his war-chief, isn't he?"

"Yeah. An' he lives up to his name, all right. That Injun's plumb loco. But he is a warrior through and through, an' kin plan a battle and carry it through like most Injun's cain't. He ain't one to cut an' run."

Bonner looked at Clint. "We cut out the stallion I wanted the other day. You can pick me six good mares. If you get them on the cars at Fort Laramie and ship them to Lincoln, I'll have my crew there to meet them. In the meantime,

Miss Somers and I can be on our way to Bismark."

"Then you'll escort me?" Her voice was noncommittal and cool. "I have no way of paying you."

"Don't worry about that," Clint said. "I'll see to your needs for the trip. If your message to Sheridan can sway him to do something about the Indian gathering, there won't be enough money in the West to pay you for what you have done."

She bowed her head. "Thank you," she whispered.

Leaving the women in the kitchen, the men left the room. On the porch they smoked and talked over plans for the shipment of the horses to Bonner's ranch, the Bar-B near Sundance, in the southern part of the Dakota Territory.

"I think, for her sake and safety, we'd better get on the way to Fort Laramie and on a train east," Bonner told Clint. "I have a feeling that she is being looked for by members of the tribe she escaped from. Most Indians

can trail a snake across a hot rock."

Clint nodded. "I'll bring her into Red Bluff this evening after dark, and you can catch tomorrow's stage to Laramie."

"I think it safer to take Clara into town after nightfall," Todd Bonner said to the mountain man, Bell. "If there is to be any danger, it would be minimized by the dark."

"Do you think the Indians have been able to track them here?" Clint asked Al Rooney. Rooney had been a Texas Ranger for several years and was known as an expert tracker, as well as one who knew his way around in a gunfight.

Al was thoughtful. He nodded. "I wouldn't be surprised if we ain't bein' watched right now, by that one she called Cold Star," he said.

"Then we'll go in at night," Bonner said firmly.

It was hard for Emmy to see Clara leave. "You get done what you have to do," Emmy kissed her cheek and whispered to her, "and come back here

to live. You are always welcome."

Clara leaned back and looked into her eyes. "You really mean that, don't you."

Emmy nodded and the two young women embraced again.

"For as long as you wish, or forever," Emmy said softly. "I have begun to think of you as the sister I never had."

"Thank you," Clara whispered. "I shall never forget you for as long as I live." But Clara was apprehensive and shivered as Emmy Steele hugged her.

"Isn't that right, Clint?" said Emmy.

"Absolutely." Clint smiled at Clara. "You are welcome here any time. There's always a place for you at our table."

"Even when you know that I have been raised by heathens?" Clara looked at both of them. "Wherever I go, even into the mercantile store, I am looked at and whispered about as that white woman who undoubtedly was taken as wife by some savage."

"Time will take care of that," said Clint earnestly. "People can be cruel and will be when they hear that about you. But you are strong and can overcome it. The loss will be theirs, not yours. You are a fine woman and Emmy and I will always be proud to call you our friend."

"You make me feel like the richest woman in the world." Clara smiled tremulously, tears filling her eyes. "I shall always remember your words and hold them in my heart."

Emmy stood beside Clint, his arm heavy on her shoulders. He knew she was sorry to see the woman leave. They had become close during the short time Clara had been in the home.

"She'll be all right," he told her softly. "Todd is not going to let anything happen to her."

Emmy shivered and huddled close to him. "I hope not," she said, her voice doubtful. "I pray not."

★ ★ ★

Bonner and Clara Somers left the horse ranch when it became full dark. He had chosen his time well, for the moon was young and did not swing high in the heavens until well up in the night. There would be minimum moonlight.

They struck a fast pace once away from the ranch. He knew Clara was a good horsewoman, having seen her ride with Emmy. She mounted firmly and moved off beside him. Her years reared with the Cheyennes and with horses had often found her astride and racing a favorite spotted pony against those of other children. Cheyenne children could usually ride a horse almost as soon as they could walk.

The trail was dark. Scudding clouds shut out starshine, and the moon was late in the sky. Trees along the trail cast deep black shadows and along one stretch there were twelve foot high cliffs on either side.

It was here Cold Star awaited them. He knew there was only one man with Girl-With-Feet-Of-Deer. He had

seen them leave the ranch, moving silently ahead of them until he saw the trail they were taking. He picked his place carefully. Surprise and instant action were the hallmarks of the Cheyenne warrior. Cold Star was considered the finest warrior among those of his tribe. He had counted many coupe, and had shed the blood of enemy warriors, more than fingers on both hands. Fellow warriors, close companions on many forages, had offered to help him find and capture Clara Somers, but he had been challenged to complete the task himself. He declined their help and now waited in the dark, atop one of the cliffs, to launch his attack in the deep shadows of the defile.

There was the soft chop-chop of hoofs in the dust of the trail. He tensed. He could see the two figures now, shadowy, moving with the motion of the horses. She turned her face and seeing her shape and form in the dark, he knew her.

They were below him, she the nearest to him. He tensed his muscles, and with a shrieking scream, cast himself headlong at her, his arms outstretched to jerk her from her horse!

4

CLINT STEELE watched Bonner and Clara Somers disappear into the darkness of the trail leading to Red Bluff. He was uneasy for some reason. The thought of only the two of them on the trail, and of the threat of danger undoubtedly hanging over the woman, stirred a caution within him.

Homer Bell, the mountain man, and Al Rooney were in the bunkhouse, playing a hand of euchre with two other hands. Clint stepped to the doorway and motioned to Bell. The huge mountain man folded his cards and came over.

"Homer, I feel a little concerned about Bonner and Clara on that trail alone. From what you told me about that warrior, Cold Star, he might have a party of his cronies out there, waiting for a chance at Clara."

The mountain man nodded. "He jist might, Clint. He's a wily critter. What you got in mind?"

Clint was silent a moment and then shrugged. "I thought maybe you and me might follow behind them a little ways until we make sure they ain't gonna be in some kind of trouble."

"I'll get the hosses saddled," Al Rooney spoke up from the darkness back of Clint. "I think I'll just join you to see what goes on."

"Fine. The three of us can follow them into Red Bluff." Clint turned to the house to inform Emmy where he was going. Al and Bell went to the corral and quickly saddled their personal mounts. When Clint came out of the house, carrying his rifle, the two men were waiting before the porch, with his horse saddled and ready. He shoved the rifle in the saddle sheath and mounted. In a moment they wheeled away from the porch and disappeared on the trail recently taken by Bonner and Clara Somers.

★ ★ ★

Philip Henry Sheridan, General, in charge of Military Operations in Western States and Territories, leaned back in his creaking chair and read for at least the tenth time the telegraph flimsy on his desk. Across from him his second in command stood at a window and looked out upon the parade ground at Fort Abraham Lincoln.

"I cannot believe that twelve thousand Sioux, Cheyennes and other tangent tribes would band together in a co-ordinated effort. It is absolutely beyond their nature to serve together in pursuit of a cause."

Colonel Randel Oates turned and looked at the general. "General, the Sioux, Cheyennes, Arapahoes, Kiowas and Utes, to mention a few, have fought each other for centuries. They are natural enemies and have battled each other over the hunting rights and portions of the plains for centuries. To bring them together for a treaty talk is

nearly impossible; for Sitting Bull to get twelve thousand of them together for a battle would be a miracle."

"Well, I'm told he's not only a chief, but a widely known and honored medicine man among the plains Indians," the general said. "Maybe he can create a miracle and bring them together." He rose to his short five feet five and walked over to the window and looked out, standing alongside his second in command. He was dark-browed, ill-tempered, hard to please by either soldier or officer. His oversized head with its shaggy, black hair nodded out at the scene.

"We have a lot of work ahead of us, and maybe a hard fight with the Indians," he told Colonel Oates. "Keep the men training and in shape. They are going to need every ounce of strength they can store up for the times ahead. I have the feeling this is going to be a long, hot summer."

★ ★ ★

As Cold Star screamed and dived from the cliff toward Clara, Bonner swerved his horse and leaped free, whirling to face the action behind him.

The Indian knocked Clara from her horse. She struck the ground on her shoulder and, ducking her head, as the Indian boys had taught her, rolled free of the horse and sprang to her feet.

Cold Star landed upon his feet and sprang toward her, seizing her about the waist and twisting to throw her over his shoulder, but the agile young woman, strong and frightened, threw her weight forward and twisted from the Indian's arms. She sprang to her feet facing him and the Indian lunged at her, his arms outstretched.

One of his arms was seized and he was thrown off-stride, and whirled about to face Todd Bonner. That the white man was armed with a six-gun and his hand was flashing down to it, was instantly caught by Cold Star. Growling with fury, he drew his knife and dived at Bonner's legs.

Todd's gun was in his hand, but Clara was just beyond the Indian and Todd hesitated to fire. The Indian slammed into his legs and Todd went down, the gun flying from his hand. Seeing it bouncing to the ground, Clara sprang and seizing it, turned to face the forms battling on the ground.

Cold Star was extremely strong. Years of training in wrestling, running and fighting had honed his body to a sharply tuned fighting machine. Todd Bonner realized this as he grappled with the Indian.

Bonner caught the Indian in the chest with both feet and the warrior flew back to bounce off the cliff side. Immediately he threw himself at the white man again, the knife flashing in the dim light of the trail. Unarmed, Todd backed away from the knife. He watched the face of the Indian, seeing the anger-twisted face, the gleaming teeth and the glittering eyes. This was a warrior closing in for the kill.

"Get down, Todd," screamed Clara.

"I'll shoot him!" At her voice the Indian whirled away from Bonner and seeing the gun in the woman's hand, yelled and threw himself at her, his knife raised to slash. She ducked his lunge and raising the six-gun fired rapidly. The blast of the gun roared in their ears in the narrow defile between the two cliffs.

Thrown off his attempt to seize her, Cold Star dived to the ground and rolled toward her, the knife raised to thrust into her lower body. Clara stepped back and stumbled, falling over a loose stone and fell, with the Indian inches away from her. She scrambled away on hands and knees, having lost the six-gun.

There was the sound of running horses. Cold Star ceased his attack on Clara and poised, listening for a quick moment. Horses were coming along the trail Todd and Clara had traveled from the ranch. He snarled and drawing back, threw the knife with all his force at the woman.

Clara flinched and ducked away, expecting to feel the cold flame of the knife entering her body. It *swished* close to her side and thudded into a treetrunk back of her. Todd rushed the Indian and tried to grapple with him, but the warrior, as was the attitude of the Indian, knew he was to be overpowered with new arrivals. He threw back his head and screamed a defiant war cry, leaped up the bank from which he had lunged earlier, and disappeared into the darkness of the forest surrounding them.

Clint Steele, followed by Bell and Rooney, came dashing up, drawing their horses to a skidding halt. "Are you all right?" called Al, his keen eyes seeing the roughed-up appearance of Bonner. Clara knelt offside, breathing deeply, holding her head in her hands. Homer Bell, thinking her hurt, dropped from his horse and went to her. "Are you hurt, Miss Clara?" he asked, his voice filled with concern.

She raised her face and looked at

him. She shook her head. "He tried to kill me," she whispered. "He came here to kill me! I have known him for over ten years — he is only three years older than me. Why he has such a hatred can only be because my adopted father refused to give me to him as his unmarried lover — his concubine."

He reached down and taking her arm, gently lifted her to her feet. "Never you mind. You ain't done nothin' to cause anybody to hate you. He's just mean, and mad because you got away from him."

"I think it's more than that," Bonner said. He stood brushing the dirt of the trail from his clothes. He had retrieved his gun from where Clara had dropped it, checked it for clogged bore and dropped it into his holster. "I think he was sent to take you, Clara. They know or suspect you heard the call to war of Sitting Bull, and are taking no chances you might pass the word along."

Bonner brought up her horse, giving her an arm up in mounting. She was

shaken, but her nerve was not gone. She nodded her thanks and settled into the saddle.

"Y'all goin' back to the ranch, or on to Red Bluff?" Clint Steele asked Bonner. Clara answered for them.

"We are going on to Red Bluff and catch the first stage to Laramie," she told Al.

"Reckon I'll just go on in with you, in case that red devil is waitin' for you somewheres up ahead," Clint said.

"I'll jist side with you fer th' ride," said Homer Bell. Todd Bonner nodded. "An' I'll come along, too," said Rooney.

"We're obliged to you for the company," he said. In a moment they rode away from the place of conflict, each lost in his own thoughts. After several minutes, Bonner called them to a halt.

"One reason the Indian was able to attack us so easily," he said, "was because we were riding so slow. We know the trail pretty well; we can see it

well enough, even though there's little light. I suggest we speed up until we are within sight of the town."

The mountain man agreed. "If we go at a gallop, he won't be apt to try another dive at Clara," he said.

"There ain't no more bluffs, like back there, fer him to jump off of," commented Al Rooney. "But a gallop is a good idea. I'd say let's get on our way."

The sound of galloping hoofs beat through the night, and Cold Star, riding above them, and thinking where he might try another attack, realized he could no longer attempt to take the white woman away from them. Sullenly he kept within sound of their passage and followed them to the edge of the town.

★ ★ ★

In the Red Bluff Hotel which boasted the best restaurant in the town, Silas Henry, Emmy Steele's father, gave

Clara the best room he had. Todd Bonner already had a room, but had planned to be leaving on the morning stage. However, Si Henry had news for Bonner that would change his plans.

They were in the small office back of the registry desk. Henry had heard the entire story of the woman and the need for her to get to Fort Abraham Lincoln, at Bismark, Dakota.

He shook his head. "You aren't going to get out of town tomorrow, Todd," he said. "A random bunch of young warriors, out to cause some excitement, I reckon, raided the way-station at High Point, and run off all the hosses. The stage is stuck there until they can get hosses across the pass to them."

Bonner was silent for a long moment, his face reflecting hard thoughts. It was important that Clara bring her report to General Sheridan, at his request, face to face. It should be as soon as humanly possible.

"No way to get horses to them in

the next couple of days?" he asked Henry.

The older man shook his head. "Nope. Nearest hosses trained to tandem to a six-hoss stage is in the main corrals for the stages half-way between here an' Fort Laramie. There's just no way to get any animals with that trainin' anywhere else."

★ ★ ★

Cold Star stood in the shadows of Harve Talbert's gun shop, across the street from the Red Bluff Hotel. He had followed Clara and her guards into town and had located where the woman was staying. He had also spoken to a crippled Ute who worked about the livery stables and learned that the stage would not be moving for several days. The white woman could not leave town.

Cold Star knew the road from Red Bluff to Fort Laramie, and the tortuous route it took in one place through

the mountain passes. He had another chance at capturing Girl-With-Feet-Of-Deer. His eyes burned with evil anger and frustration. She would be his to do with as he pleased before many more hours passed!

5

CLARA SOMERS stood at a window in the Red Bluff Hotel and looked out upon the main thoroughfare of the town, named Main Street for the obvious reason it was the only complete street running east and west through the town. All other streets fed into it, alleys opened on to it, and both ends of Main Street became a trail that led away into the distance. The eastern end left the town and gradually angled south toward Laramie. The western leg wandered away out over the plain and finally became a narrow road leading through a low pass toward other higher peaks.

She was apprehensive, shaken by her encounter with Cold Star, the Cheyenne warrior who had lusted after her as his concubine. She knew him from her youth growing up in the village

of Buffalo Man, the old chief who had mainly ignored her. Her adoptive father, One-Who-Leaps-Highest, had protected her mainly because of the need of her strong body to do the work of Red Leaf, his wife who was very ill when Clara was captured and brought to them by their son as a slave.

Cold Star had been a member of the youth who teased the nubile girls of the camp. His early animosity toward Clara began when she refused his erotic advances at the age of fourteen. Later she outran him in a contest which involved the teenage youth of the camp. She had beaten everyone in other contests. He was three years her senior and blustered that Girl-With-Feet-Of-Deer could never beat him in a dash laid out along the perimeter of the camp.

On the day of the race she out-distanced him handily and the young men and maidens of the camp teased and jeered at his letting a white-eye girl outrun him. From that time on he

was her enemy, and tried to embarrass her, or harm her in some minor way. The final chastisement was his when One-Who-Leaps-Highest, her adoptive father, refused to let him have Clara as a bed-mate.

All this ran through her mind as she looked out on to the night-shrouded street. She knew Cold Star well, and did not doubt that he was out there now, and knew where she was. She shivered, clasping her arms about her front. Would she ever be free of his clutches?

The thought of Todd Bonner came to her mind. Tall, silent, with deep-green eyes that seemed to see and know everything that moved around him. Emmy Steele had told her he was the owner of a ranch in the Dakota territories and had come to Red Bluff as a United States federal marshal looking for a man who had murdered his best friend.

A gunfighter? He had killed men. She shuddered. So much killing. The

warriors of the tribe where she had grown up spent hours bragging about their coupe, and about the enemy they had killed in their frequent rampages against other tribes, or against the white man.

Undoubtedly Todd Bonner had been a soldier, for he carried an air of command and maintained an erect stance that bespoke of the military. Perhaps one day he would tell her about that, and about himself and his ranch. Emmy had not said whether he was married, or if he had children. The subject might have come to Clara's mind, but she had never spoken of it.

What was it like to have a husband? To give him children? What was it to be in love with a man? In love enough to give him your time, your lovingness, your body to bear children? A hint of wonder ran through her mind. Was she falling in love with this man? She had never thought about another male in such a way. Suddenly her face was hot and a strange feeling crept through

her. She felt heavy in the loins and her breath was suddenly faster.

She shook her head to clear it. Foolishness, she thought. He is probably married and has a dozen kids running around that ranch of his. Get your head together, Clara Somers, Girl-With-Feet-Of-Deer. You never fell in love with any of the fine, handsome young warriors in the tribe. Why this man now?

Still, her mind told her, he is helping you in a very important task and . . . it is nice to think about a man, finally, of your own race.

She shook her head and smiled to herself. Grow up, Clara Somers, she mused. Then the thought came to her . . . what if he isn't married! The wonderful feeling ran through her again and she sat down upon the edge of the bed, then lay back, her head on the pillow, and let the mysterious wonder of it lull her into thoughts cherished by womanhood since the beginning of time.

* * *

Todd Bonner stood at a window of his room. He lit a slim, dark cigar and puffed it, savoring the aromatic flavor. It was hard to come by a good cigar out here beyond the edge of civilization. This one had been handed him by the mayor of Red Bluff in gratitude of tasks done for the town's good in past weeks.

But his thoughts were not upon tobacco and the pleasure of its taste. He thought of Clara Somers. He smiled to himself. The Indians had a way of naming individuals according to their abilities. He could tell by the way she carried her rather tall, lean body, that she could very well be Girl-With-Feet-Of-Deer. And she could indeed ride a horse, astride, very well. Her years with the tribe had left her with certain important skills.

And did I say tall and *lean*? he thought. During the few days at the Steele ranch he had observed her from

time to time, and saw the fullness of womanhood in her body, soft breasts pressing against the fabric of her dress, the slim waist and the ripeness of hips, the depth of body that spoke of the richness of womanhood.

He stirred uneasily. It had been a long, lonely three years since Nina had died in his arms. She had given birth to their second child, a girl. The first, a son, Adam, was thriving and growing and Nina had wanted another child . . . a baby to hold and love and cuddle, she had wheedled him.

He sighed. The doctor had warned them that it would be dangerous to have another child, but the pulse of mothering beat heavily and she became pregnant. It was a long, difficult birth. Sadness crossed his features, as he stared into the street and remembered it. The baby came healthy and protesting its entrance into this place of motion and noise. But the struggle to bring the little daughter into the world was too much for her body.

Nina died three days later, holding her baby to her breast in her last gesture of motherhood.

He shook his head. Such memories were painful. He had seldom thought of another woman. Nina had filled his life with her smile, her strength and her loving. He would never find another such, yet . . . Adam was five, soon to be six, and little Amanda was three. His foreman's wife was caring for them in his absence. He missed them so, their smiles, their rushing to him. He missed the touch of a loving woman, warm arms, warm kisses . . .

Why am I thinking like this? he mused. Does the sight of a young woman such as Clara Somers trigger such emotions? He had been aware of the inviting glances of women since Nina had died. There was a widow or two in Sundance who made certain their baskets at church socials were marked so he could identify them, should he wish to bid upon them. But none of these had stirred him as

did the presence of the young woman who was depending upon him for her safety on a long trip . . . together.

He stood for a long time looking out of the window, his thoughts wandering. He noted the passage of an old Indian who worked at the stables, ambling along the boardwalk heading toward the Open Door Saloon. Just another on the streets late at night.

He finally turned back into the room and, undressing, lay upon the bed. His mind kept busy; it was a long time before sleep claimed him.

★ ★ ★

Cold Star, after watching the hotel for several hours, silently left the town, his presence there and his departure unknown. With the knowledge that the stage would not come into the town and leave for at least three or four days, he raced toward his village.

There would be a way for him to seize the white woman. He would bring

young warrior friends and together they would capture her and take her back to the village of Buffalo Man. Whoever was with her, thinking they would keep her from him would be greatly surprised!

6

THE council held in Buffalo Man's hogan was made up of the elders of the tribe, plus the war chief, Cold Star and the adoptive father of Girl-With-Feet-Of-Deer. Cold Star had related his attempt to capture the girl and his being thwarted by the approach of several white-eyes with many guns. But he knew where the girl was being taken and how. It would be an easy matter for him and a few warriors to capture her and bring her to the village to stand before Buffalo Man and his council.

"I seem to recall these were the words of this man when he left the village five days ago, 'it would be easy to capture and bring this girl before the council'." The chief turned his eyes upon members of the council. "Or is there an echo in the hogan, remaining

all those days just now to return."

Cold Star's face tightened in anger. "I will capture this girl, with the warriors helping me with the stage and those who will be guarding its passage," he said stiffly. "My words are still good. I have but to change my plans for a better one."

"Are we to assume that Cold Star has such a plan?" Buffalo Man levered his black, glittering gaze at the young warrior. "It seems your plans have been like the tumbleweed that goes before the wind and lands wherever it will, without aim or purpose. If you have a good plan, we will listen; if you are just casting thoughts like a foolish woman, then leave us. We have other important things to discuss."

Cold Star stood stiff and tall before his chief. Buffalo Man was greatly respected among the Cheyenne. His coups were without number, and scalps festooned the door frame of his lodge. Cold Star knew he had to present his ideas firmly and without

hesitation from beginning to end. His eyes fastened on those of his chief, he began to outline his plan to capture Girl-With-Feet-Of-Deer.

★ ★ ★

Silas Henry, the hotel owner, came from the lobby to the veranda, where Todd Bonner leaned against one of the posts. The older man tamped loose-cut tobacco into the bowl of his ripely aromatic pipe and lit it with a match. Once he had it going he nodded to Todd.

"I talked with the livery men early this morning," he said. "There was a six-hoss team delivered to the stage station yesterday. The stage should be along in another day. I guess this has slowed down your plans some, huh?"

Todd nodded. "Yes, some. I wanted to get on the way the day after we got in town. But stolen horses have to be replaced and like most other things, that takes time."

Clara Somers came from the lobby and smiled at the men. "I haven't had breakfast yet, I wonder if two handsome men would like to join me?"

Silas Henry winked at Todd. "Well, the handsome part leaves me out, and I have just finished breakfast, so I'll take a rain check on that, Miss Somers. Thank you, anyway."

"And you?" Clara cocked a dark eyebrow at Bonner. "Have you eaten yet?"

"Miss Somers," Bonner said, sweeping off his hat and bowing in a grandiose gesture, "if I had eaten two breakfasts, I would still accept your invitation and eat another. But, no, I have not eaten, and yes, I will be delighted to accept your invitation. May I escort you to the dining-room?"

Clara laughed, her voice a happy lilt and Silas Henry chuckled. "Now, that was about the most grand acceptance I have seen in my days. Enjoy your meal, young people. This old man has work to do." He tipped his hat to Clara,

and walked away shaking his head and chuckling.

The dining-room was not busy. It was a little later than most diners appeared. Business men had eaten and left to open their doors. Here and there guests of the hotel were chatting over a last cup of coffee. It was a quiet, pleasant room, with the attractive odor of brewing coffee coming from the kitchen.

Bonner escorted Clara to a table to one side of the dining-room and, pulling out a chair, seated her. Clara noted, with understanding, that he took a chair with his back to the wall. She had watched Indian men, wary of enemies, sit with such caution, their eyes moving, their backs protected from some real or imagined enemy. It startled her somewhat to see it occurring here, in what she considered civilization. She had not been away from the Indian culture long enough yet to realize that what she considered wondrous in Red Bluff, was actually

the edge of encroaching civilization. It would take years before the culture of America beyond the Mississippi River became a reality in the deep western territories and states.

The waitress came and took their orders, Bonner's a hearty meal with steak and potatoes, biscuits and red-eye gravy, with a continuously replenished mug of coffee. She ordered more lightly with pancakes, syrup, biscuits and jelly, with the coffee.

"You are very kind to offer to escort me to Bismark," she told him softly.

"Don't mention it," he said, smiling. "It isn't often a rough rancher like me gets the opportunity to spend several days in the company of a pretty young woman."

She blushed and lowered her eyes. When she looked up and started to speak, the waitress was there with their meal. Whatever she was about to say was left unsaid. Perhaps for the better, she thought to herself. For she was about to ask him if he was

married and if so, about his wife and children. The business of eating, passing the salt, pepper and sugar, and other material for the meal, made up the content of their conversation. It was pleasant and she found herself relaxing, totally enjoying the moment and his company.

"Are you Bonner?" a rough, gravelly voice cut through the course of their quiet talk. Todd quietly laid down his fork and slowly wiped his mouth with the napkin before he looked up at the man, standing threateningly before their table. Others in the room had noticed the attitude of the man and his stance and the buzz of casual talk through the room began to quieten.

"I'm Bonner," replied Todd. The man before him was tall, running to fat around the middle. About his belly was strapped a gunbelt holding a low-slung calibre .44. The man's hands, however, were a different thing. They were slender, well-cared for, Todd quickly noted, and on the right hand

was a soft, leather glove. A shooter, thought Todd. And he's after me. How did he learn I once was a gunnie? None of this showed on his taciturn features, as his green eyes narrowed and met the glower of the other's gaze.

"I'm Harve Quincy," the man said, his voice rasping as though from a sore throat. "So you're a United States marshal, huh?"

"I was," replied Bonner quietly.

"Was? You ain't now? Well, now, that's just about right. I guess the gov'ment wouldn't care about their deputies runnin' around with an Injun squaw."

Clara gasped and for the first time glanced up at the man. His thick lips leered down at her and he reached as though to touch her shoulder. She drew back from him and looked at Bonner.

Bonner's face tightened in anger. "I don't know who you are, mister. But you have just insulted a lady, a white lady, but Indian or white, you are way out of line."

"I don't reckon I am," Quincy sniggered. "I wonder if these here people in here realize they are eatin' in the same room with a woman who was livin' with an Injun buck a week or so ago?"

The room was completely still, all eyes on the table at one side of the room. Bonner pushed back his chair and stood up. "I will meet you outside, mister, whoever you are. You have just bought yourself a bunch of trouble."

"Oh, Todd, don't . . . let it go," Clara said softly. "I don't care what he thinks or cares about me."

Bonner did not look at her. "I care," he said, his voice cool as tinkling ice.

He moved toward the man causing the trouble. "I don't want any trouble here in this room. Someone besides you might get hurt. But, mister, you *are* going to be hurt!"

He stepped around the man, turning his back upon him, walked toward the lobby of the hotel, his stride measured and sure. Silas Henry appeared in the

doorway and looked at him. Seeing the fury in Bonner's eyes, he knew something was wrong, and stepped aside, seeing the stranger following his friend with a sneer upon his face.

As Bonner stepped out on to the street porch Henry gestured to the clerk at the desk. "Run and get Sheriff Topp," he said. "There's a heap of trouble coming our way." The clerk stared at him and then, dropping his pen on the desk, ran out of a side door which led to the main street.

Bonner preceded the man through the doorway of the hotel. As Quincy stepped out upon the porch, Bonner whirled and drew his gun. One moment his hand was empty, the next moment it was nudging the soft belly of the stranger. The man grunted and stepped back, his face flushing with anger.

"Sneaky, ain't you?" he growled.

"Raise your right hand," gritted Bonner, his green eyes sparkling ice in his face. "Slow and easy now, undo your gunbelt with your left

hand." He cocked his six-gun and the man paled somewhat as he heard the ominous *click*.

He did as Bonner bid and the gunbelt with the heavy six-gun dropped to the boards with a thump.

"Now, walk out into the street, mister. We'll see if we can teach you some manners." Bonner watched the man walk down the steps and turn about ten feet from the porch. Quincy stood sneering at Bonner.

"D'you think you kin whup me? Bare fist? I'll eat you alive, spit you out an' then go take keer of yore squaw filly."

Bonner unbelted his gun and handed it to Silas Henry who had appeared in the doorway. Without answering the man he stepped out into the street and approached him, his stride lithe, his eyes never leaving the man's face.

Suddenly Quincy lurched forward, his fists whirling through the air before him. Apparently he had had his turn at street and barroom fighting, for as he

got within range he swung a haymaker right at Bonner, and kicked out at the same time Bonner sidestepped both attempts. As the man whirled slipping past him, he slammed a right fist into the kidney area. The man grunted and staggered. Catching his balance he turned and launched himself at Bonner, his face purple with rage and frustration.

Bonner met him squarely and the two men traded blows, the sound of fists meeting flesh slapping echoes against the buildings. A fist caught Bonner on the temple and he saw stars, as he slammed to the dirt of the street. Knowing the man would attempt to stomp him, he rolled as he hit and came to his knees in time to meet a roundhouse blow that sent him rolling in the street once more.

Leaping into the air Quincy attempted to land on Bonner with both feet, but the smaller man slipped away and was again on his feet. As the man turned to him again Bonner was right there,

and found his chin with an uppercut that had started at his knees.

Quincy staggered, his eyes blurred. Bonner bored in, lefts and rights slamming into the soft belly and face, finding the chin again. The man back-pedaled to get away from Bonner's flurry of blows. He was weakening. With his size so much more than that of Bonner, he had thought to finish the fight quickly. But it was a different story.

The big man rallied momentarily and traded blows again with Bonner. But Bonner was finding his second wind. His green eyes glinting and narrowed, he moved inside the big man's weakening swings and again his right fist pounded the chin. Quincy staggered, now gasping for breath.

Stalking him, as a cat stalks its prey, Bonner moved in on the man, cutting, slashing with devastating accuracy. Quincy moved back and back until his ankles were against the boardwalk before the general store. A crowd had

gathered and moved along with the action, amazed that Bonner could make such a fight against such a tremendously large man.

Bonner drew back his right fist. With all the accumulated strength of his shoulders, upper chest and arms, made solid and strong with years of work, he launched a blow that almost whistled in its intensity. It struck the man in the center of his chest, over the heart; his left fist lashed in and sank into the soft belly above the belt and again a tremendous right cross-slugged into the chin, with a soggy, meaty sound.

Quincy's eyes glazed, his mouth opened and poured blood as he gasped for breath. He staggered and his feet stumbled over the boardwalk and he fell, the dust rising from the boards as his weight slammed into them. He groaned and rolled over and sat up, holding his head in his hands, blood dripping on to the boards beneath him.

Bonner stood over him for a moment,

weariness seeping into his muscles. He was breathing heavily and his knuckles were bleeding from the pounding they had taken. His chest and arms were aching from the hammering blows of the man's huge fists. Bonner stood straight and alert, watching the man.

Seeing there was no more fight in the drooping hulk before him, Bonner walked back to the porch. Clara stood in the doorway, one hand over her mouth, her eyes following Bonner's approach. As Bonner stepped up on the porch, Silas Henry handed him his gunbelt. Bonner looked up into Clara's face as he swung the belt about his waist, and settled the gun in place.

"I'm sorry I . . . caused you so much trouble," she whispered. She reached out and touched a darkening bruise on his face.

"For the reason it was done," he told her soberly, "no need for being sorry. You have every right to have someone protect you from such scum."

Roy Topp, the Red Bluff marshal,

moved over to him. "I just got here, Bonner, but you seem to have taken pretty good care of the situation — "

"*Bonner!*"

The yell echoed down the street. The marshal turned as did Bonner toward the source.

"Oh, no!" The marshal saw the hulking form of the man Bonner had just whipped, swaying in the street. In his hand was a six-gun. He had lumbered to his feet and as a cowboy moved by him, curiously looking at him, he had seized the man, slapped him back and snatched the gun from his holster.

"I'm gonna kill you, Bonner! You killed my friend, Lear Holbrook, an' I'm gonna even the score."

"That's what it is all about," murmured Bonner. He stepped down from the porch, angling out into the street until those on the porch were safe from any stray bullets.

"Leave it be, mister," he said. "It's all over. Holbrook paid his dues. He

was a murderer and I was acting as a lawman so just leave it there. You go your way and I'll go mine." Bonner moved slowly toward the man, his eyes never leaving the clawed right fingers of his opponent.

"Holbrook and me went back a long way. I aim to kill you for what you done."

Bonner came to a halt. Quincy held the gun before him, his rage making it waver and tremble in his hand. He pointed it in Bonner's direction, swaying in his anger and frustration at having been physically beaten by this man before him. A gunman with his own reputation, he could not let it lie.

Bonner knew it was useless to argue with Quincy. He saw Roy Topp move in to his right. The town marshal called to the man with the gun.

"Quincy, toss your gun over to the side of the street and be done with this. I won't arrest you. You can get on your horse and leave town — "

"No two-bit lawman in a flea-bit

town like this can tell me what to do. You just stay outa this. It's none of your business." Quincy did not even look at the marshal.

"He won't listen to you, Roy," Bonner said quietly. "Let him do his thing."

The marshal hesitated and then moved to one side, his eyes fastened upon the big man.

Quincy crouched. The gun now dangled beside his right leg. Bonner stood quietly, his hands at his side, his green eyes narrowed, watching the expression on Quincy's face.

The big man growled and his hand moved up swiftly, his thumb cocking the gun as it came level. Suddenly it was no longer trembling and wavering. The instincts of a practised gunslinger had taken over.

There was a blast of fire leaping from the muzzle of his gun and the slug whistled past Bonner's ear. Only then did Bonner move.

His gun hand blurred down and up

and the gun in his fingers roared! Quincy screamed and staggered back and then the crowd watching stood with mouths gaping and eyes widening in surprise.

Quincy was holding his gun hand and moaning with pain. The hand was mangled and pouring blood. Bonner's bullet had struck the weapon and blasted it from Quincy's hand, taking some of his fingers with it. The man fell to his knees, squeezing his right wrist, and writhing in pain. He raised his pain-filled eyes to Bonner and cursed him vilely.

"I'll be back, Bonner! I'll find you and kill you if it's the last thing I ever do," he screamed.

Bonner calmly punched out the empty shells from his six-gun and reloaded it from shells in his gunbelt. He did not answer the man, but turned and spoke to the marshal.

"Better get him to the doctor, Roy, before he bleeds to death," he said.

"Or talks hisself to death," a bearded

bystander said. "Say, that was real shootin', Bonner. Real good."

Bonner nodded curtly and stepped up on the hotel porch. He went to Clara and reaching out, took her hand.

"Don't you blame yourself at all for this. Quincy used you as a way of getting at me for a personal grudge. I'm just sorry you were insulted as you were." He looked earnestly into her eyes.

"I don't worry about being called names," she murmured. She touched his face again, oblivious to those about who saw her. "I'm just sorry you were hurt on my behalf."

Silas Henry broke in, "I didn't get a chance to tell you that feller had been askin' about you," he told Bonner. "But anyway you took care of him. With any luck, you'll be outa here on the stage tomorrow."

7

THE stage road from Red Bluff was rough and winding, rising into the foothills of Elk Mountains. The vehicle was pulled by six horses, all experienced animals in this work. The driver was Nat Billings, a veteran of the Civil War and years driving wagons and stages over the sometimes almost impassable roads. On the seat beside him was Burt Holden, riding shotgun, although it had been some time since there had been any problems with wily Indian bucks out to harass some white-eyes, or road agents hoping to lift an army payroll. Nevertheless, Holden kept a wary eye on areas where trouble might lurk.

Silas Henry had helped Bonner and Clara Somers on to the stage with their bags.

"You oughta get to the fort without

any trouble," he said. "There's only one place where anyone might try to stop the stage on this road. It's a low pass crossing from this range over on to the stretch into the fort. However, Holden knows the road and he'll be on the lookout."

Bonner and Clara were joined on the stage by an individual dressed in black coat, pants and tie, with a gleaming white shirt. He wore a narrow-brimmed black hat and was clean shaven except for a drooping moustache. His eyes, a pale grey, surveyed them coolly. He nodded, touched his hat-brim to Clara with a finger, and settled back, ignoring them, looking out of the window of the stage.

Bonner looked him over quickly and recognized the traditional garb of the gambler who traveled the west, one town to another, never settling long in one place. He also noted a bulge under the man's coat on the left side. The man carried a gun.

"There's no rest stops 'til we get to

the way-station, just before we climb the pass over the Elks," the driver had informed Bonner. "We change hosses there an' you kin get a bite to eat, if you kin tolerate what old Miz Crawford puts on the table. She just ain't the best cook in Wyoming Territory."

Clara laughed. "By that time we may be so hungry that anything will taste good," she said.

They sat side by side on the hard seat facing forward. The gambler sat across from Bonner, but aside from the first nod of the head, there had been no communication between them.

"I have been all over these mountains," Clara murmured to Bonner. "My tribe moved as the seasons changed. A deep valley away from the winds further south, where the sun kept us warm. Game was plentiful there, and we ate good. Deer, elk and now and then a *Pte* — buffalo, in English — "

The man across from them turned his head quickly and looked at Clara. "How is it you speak the language of

The People," he asked her in swift, articulate Cheyenne.

Clara stared at him in shock. Bonner's green eyes narrowed. Clara looked at Bonner and then at the man again and answered him in Cheyenne. "I was the adopted daughter of a Cheyenne sub-chief for many years."

"And how come you can speak the tongue so fluently?" asked Bonner of the man.

There was no friendliness on the face of the man. "That is none of your business. I am speaking to the young lady," he told Bonner.

"I'm making it my business," said Bonner. "The young lady is with me. I'll ask you again what you asked her. How come you speak Cheyenne so well?"

"Are you part Indian?" asked Clara, speaking in English this time. The man shook his head, his eyes never leaving her face.

"I was a fur trader for many years among the Northern Cheyenne," he

told her. "I learned the tongue from trading and hunting with them. I spent many years among them." He nodded at the mountain foothills outside the stage which they were now climbing.

"If you lived among the Elk Mountains and in this part of Wyoming Territory," he continued, "then you must have been with the tribe of Buffalo Man. He has been the leading Cheyenne chief in this area for many years."

"A fur trader never dressed in black suit and white starched shirt," Bonner observed dryly. "You have made a great change from buffalo hides and wolf skins to broadcloth and linen."

The man nodded and for the first time a frosty smile moved his lips under the drooping moustache. "A long ways from the rendezvous to being gambling-hall dealer," he said. "But change is what makes the world go around." He paused and then added, "I'd say you are making a change of some sort, riding this rough stage from somewhere to somewhere."

Bonner simply looked at the man. Clara looked out of the window again. The man stared hard at them for a long moment and then he lapsed into his customary silence. Outside the coach, Nat Billings yelled at his wheelers and snapped his whip over their backs. Burt Holden spat a squirt of tobacco juice over the front wheel and continued his eying the terrain about them. The vehicle bounced and creaked, the horses flung their weight into the harness and pounded the hard road with iron-shod hoofs. Miles passed beneath the wheels and coming to a creek ford, Billings slowed the stage to a crawl.

Crossing the ford, Burt Holden was alert and wary. He clutched his double-barrelled shotgun tightly, and eyed every tree surrounding the crossing. All was quiet and he spoke to the driver.

"I think it's safe to stop and rest the horses when we get across," he said. "If we was goin' to be jumped, they'd have done it by now."

Pulling out of the ford, Billings circled the stage around on a shaded flat to one side of the road. There he told the passengers they might dismount and rest their legs while he rested the horses.

Clara and Bonner wandered down to the stream and stood talking quietly, watching the flowing water and listening to its melodic murmuring over the stones. The passenger in black watched them and then, finding a tree to lean against, he lit a pipe and smoked, standing in solitude away from the others.

"I wonder who he is," Clara murmured to Bonner, seeing the man by himself. "He never gave his name nor did he ask ours," she commented.

Bonner shrugged. "A traveling gambler, by his clothes, and tight-mouthed about himself. Could be he left some town with trouble nagging his heels. The further he can get with the least amount of recognition, the better for him."

"He spoke Cheyenne perfectly," she said.

"There are white men who can speak the Indian tongue well, whichever tribe they had experience with along the way. It isn't rare, but not usual."

She sighed and looked at him. "How long will it be before we are in Bismark?" It was the first time she had questioned the distance. Up to now she had accepted the fact of the passage of miles and time without comment.

Bonner was thoughtful. "From Fort Laramie to Lincoln by train will take a week. From there by stage to Bismark and to Fort Abraham Lincoln, where we'll find Sheridan, no doubt, is another story. It will be over three hundred miles by stage to Bismark. Call it another three or four weeks. So we will be a good month from Bismark when we board the train at Fort Laramie."

She shuddered. "So far, and if all stages are as comfortable as this one, I dread to think of it."

"You can back out and we can telegraph Sheridan again," he suggested. "You can rest up with Emmy and Clint Steele and make up your mind what you want to do."

Before she could answer, the stage driver hailed them. "Hosses is rested enough, folks. Hope you are too. It's time to hit the trail."

As they walked back to the stage she clung to his arm. "I want to face Sheridan with this information. He doesn't believe what we told him in the first telegram. He won't believe another." They were at the stage. The man in black entered before them and as Bonner handed Clara up the steps, she paused and looked at him.

"You will be with me? All the way?"

He nodded. "Yes, Clara. Every step, every mile of the way." She smiled at him and squeezed his hand and stepped up into the vehicle.

* * *

The pass over Elk Mountain was one of the lower passes in the area. It had been used for centuries. First by the early arrivals, ancestors to the present-day Indians, whom they called 'The Old People', or 'they Who Come Before'.

Indians had worn the trail smooth through the centuries, before the white man appeared upon it. Explorers of the Rocky Mountains, following the Lewis and Clark expedition, found the pass. Captains of wagon trains, leading settlers towards their golden dreams of California, used it.

Where the pass levered out at the crest, before beginning the descent that would lead down to rolling plains and south-east to Fort Laramie, it was relatively flat and smooth. On either side of the trail were rocky flats before the slopes began to rise toward peaks. Here on these flats were pull-offs, where the travelers rested their teams. A small stream dived down from one mountain slope, became a creek that formed a gentle bend on one flat

beyond the trail, before leaping off into some unknown valley beyond.

In some millennium, when the earth belched and rolled, and these peaks thrust up from its molten bowels, giant boulders had been heaved upward and left tumbled to one side of what finally became a pass through the mountains. Here, hidden from the trail, but watching the approach of the stage, waited Cold Star and six young bucks, personal friends, former companions in other forays against traditional Indian enemies or the hated 'white-eyes'.

Bonner was uneasy. He simply could not believe that the Indian, Cold Star, wishing so vehemently to capture Clara Somers, would not attack the stage somewhere along the trail. Not being from this area, unacquainted with the terrain, Bonner had no way or presuming where or when the attack might come.

Reaching the crest of the pass, the stage driver swung the stage from the trail, circled beneath a copse of

jackpines and scrub oak, and pulled the horses to a halt. He leaned down from the seat and yelled to the passengers.

"Y'all kin get out an' stretch yore legs agin. This'll be the last stop until we get to the way-station, about half-way to the fort. Better take advantage of it."

He clambered down from the high seat, followed by the shotgun rider, and wandered away from the stage into a clump of trees and bushes.

Clara stirred as though to dismount. Bonner took hold of her arm and held her. "Wait a few minuses," he said softly. "It might be better."

She gave him a questioning glance and settled down beside him again, her hand comfortably upon his arm. The man in black looked at Bonner.

"Do you suspect trouble here?"

Bonner shook his head. "Can't say I do. But this would be a mightily convenient place for an ambush, now, wouldn't it?"

The stranger looked out of the stage

window and nodded. "Very much so," he agreed.

"We haven't introduced ourselves," Clara said to the man. "I am Clara Somers, and you were right, I have lived over ten years in Buffalo Man's camp."

He nodded. "I figured that, since you knew this area so well." He looked at Bonner with raised eyebrows. "I'm Ben Thompson," he said simply.

Bonner looked at him quizzically. "Strange to see you here, Mr Thompson. I heard you were killed in New Mexico two years ago."

Thompson shrugged. "I read an eastern writer recently who said that 'the report of his demise was greatly exaggerated'. I guess it's the same with me."

Bonner reached over his hand. "I'm Todd Bonner, Mr Thompson. From the Dakotas. Miss Somers and I are on our way back there on business."

"Bonner, Bonner? That Bonner . . . the nephew of John Wesley Hardin?"

101

Before the rancher could answer, there was a scream from without the stage. Bonner thrust his head out of the window in time to see the stage driver rush from the bushes, and fall, two arrows sticking from his back, quivering in the hot sun.

Shrill whoops and yips came to them and Thompson swore. "We've got some Injuns whooping right at us." His six-gun appeared from beneath his arm and he thrust it from the window on his side and fired. He threw open the door and leaped from the stage to fall beneath the swinging club of a mounted buck, whose painted face screamed defiance and hatred.

Clara screamed and crouched back against the seat. The door crashed open on her side and Bonner fired directly into the body of a young warrior who attempted to seize Clara and drag her from the coach.

The horses were down, dead from shots fired into their brains, screaming their lives out as lances and arrows

were thrust or released close up into their bodies. The bucks swarmed about the coach shrilling their voices and ducking as Bonner emptied his guns at their dodging, gyrating figures.

Suddenly the entire company of Indians gathered to one side of the stage and began to pepper the vehicle with arrows and thrown lances. Like their leader, Cold Star, they carried no white-man guns. The only weapon spitting fire was that of Todd Bonner, and he knew that he would soon be out of shells.

The band of bucks began screaming and yelling and rushed the stage in a group. Bonner threw himself to the window of the stage and levered his gun to fire when the door opposite him was again jerked open. He whirled and met the blunt end of a club in the fist of Cold Star. Bonner fell between the stage seats, dazed and bleeding.

Yelling in defiance and triumph, Cold Star seized Clara and jerked her from the stage. She struggled and

fought him, striking and scratching. Deliberately he struck her in the neck with the club and she fell into his arms unconscious.

Cold Star threw her across his horse in front of him, and directed one of his men to pull Bonner from the coach and bring him along. This done, the remaining Indians, some of them wounded and bleeding, dashed up a ravine back of the huge boulders and in a moment were gone from the scene.

Cold Star was triumphant! He had Girl-With-Feet-Of-Deer at his whim and desire! Now Buffalo Man would see whether he was as a foolish woman, he thought. And also he had captured a white-eye male to bring sport to the village.

★ ★ ★

The marauding bucks were gone. The flats at the crest of the pass became still. Bird sounds, frightened to silence during the furious attack, the screams

of the men and horses, began again. Rodents, huddled in holes and crevices, came out cautiously and then, finding the frightening noises and activity gone, began their daily food hunts.

The black-clad figure, sprawled beneath the stage, stirred. Ben Thompson, gunslinger, lawman at times, owl-hoot trail rider at other times, and presently a gambler, cautiously levered himself on an elbow and surveyed the scene.

Dazed and hurt by the blow on the shoulder and head from a warclub, Thompson had managed to wriggle beneath the protective bulk of the stage and lay, as dead, for the rest of the time. His gun emptied and having no more shells, he had lain quietly and watched as the woman and Bonner were tossed on the horses and carried away. He had waited a long half-hour before stirring.

Groaning with pain, he pulled himself from beneath the vehicle and clutching a wheel, pulled himself erect. His head throbbed. Blood had seeped down his

neck and over his black coat from the gash in his scalp. Otherwise he found himself unhurt. Slowly he made his way to the front of the stage and was startled. One horse was unhurt.

Jerked off its feet by the other animals as they fell and struggled, one of the wheelers had escaped injury. Working carefully, Thompson released the animal from the tangled harness and urging it to its feet, led it away from the blood scent of its dead companions.

He gentled the animal and leading it to the small creek, let it drink its fill. There was no saddle, but there was a lead-line and a soft length of a well-used lariat in the boot of the stage. From this he fashioned a hackamore.

Talking gently to the horse, he led it to the stage and standing upon the lower step, mounted the animal. He winced at the thought of long miles bareback through the mountains, but there was no other recourse.

Clucking to the horse, he turned it and began his journey down the

mountain, back to Red Bluff, where a telegram relating the Indian raid could be sent to Fort Laramie, alerting the army to the situation.

Grimacing, he heeled the horse into a slow trot, and without looking back, left the scene. There, for a few furious minutes, the red-man and white-man had again clashed in their ongoing battles for these lands.

8

ROY TOPP, sheriff of Red Bluff, Wyoming, looked out of the open door of his office as he heard a horse pull up before the hitch-rail in front. He was rising from his chair back of the desk when boots scraped on the boardwalk and the bulk of a man filled the open doorway.

He was not a large man, but it seemed to the sheriff at the moment that something had used him in a big way. He was bedraggled, a black coat was ripped and dirty. A once white shirt was soiled and grey with trail dust. The man stood and looked at him with tired eyes.

"Is there something I can do for you?" asked Topp.

The man entered the room and lowered himself gingerly into a straight chair before the sheriff's desk.

"Yes, Sheriff, there is. The stage was attacked by a band of Indian bucks at the top of Elk Mountain pass. The driver and shotgun rider are dead, and a Mr Bonner and a Miss Clara Somers were captured and carried away."

The sheriff stared at him, his mouth open. "An Indian attack? Why, there's been no trouble — "

"There's trouble now, Sheriff," the man interrupted. "A girl captured, a man captured either alive or dead, and I can't vision them bothering to carry away a dead man. Two others dead. Yes, there's trouble now."

"And you escaped?" There was a question in the sheriffs voice.

"I was clubbed and left for dead," the man replied. "I came to and rolled under the stage just as they finished up and pulled out."

The sheriff rose. "I have to send a telegram to Fort Laramie. They've been trying to get old Buffalo Man to take his tribe into the reservation at Fort Robinson, but he's argued and

109

delayed. I'll bet they shove them all on to the reservation now, and right away."

He hesitated at the door. "You're lucky, mister. Say, I never even asked your name." He turned and looked at the tired man in the chair.

"Ben Thompson," the man said shortly. "I rode a horse bareback all the way from the pass. My rear is raw, I'm as tired as I have ever been in my life — point me to a hotel and a bath."

Topp nodded. "Thompson, eh? We'll talk later. Don't leave town until." He pointed down the street. "The Red Bluff Hotel is run by Silas Henry. Go tell him I sent you. He'll fix up a bath for you." Topp turned and hurried from the room and down the street to the small telegraph office.

★ ★ ★

The sheriff was in his office, awaiting a reply from his telegram to Fort

Laramie. He was waiting until the answer came before seeking out Thompson to question him further. He knew the reputation of the gunman and gambler and was none too happy to have him in Red Bluff. Clint Steele and Todd Bonner had cleaned the rough element from Red Bluff recently and wrested control of the area from a range hog, Lear Holbrook, who had been a wanted murderer. The sheriff had had his fill of these characters who lived by the gun. Ben Thompson had such a reputation and Topp would breathe easier when the man was gone from the town.

He looked up from a sheaf of wanted posters as the mountain man, Homer Bell, came through the door.

The huge man paused and looked at the sheriff. "Do I hear it right? A bunch of young bucks jumped the stage and carried off Clara and Bonner?"

Topp nodded. "That's the report I got from a fellow who lived through the raid and managed to get back here with the news."

Bell was silent for a moment. "Musta been that Cold Star and some of his bucks. That'd mean he probably took them to Buffalo Man's village. Where kin I find this feller, I'd like to talk to him a leetle."

"I sent him down to the hotel for a room and a bath," said the sheriff. "He's probably chin deep in a tub of suds about now."

"I'm goin' to have a conflab with him." Bell moved towards the door. "D'ya think the army will try to get Bonner and Girl-With-Feet-Of-Deer back?" He used Clara Somers' Cheyenne name.

"I don't know, Homer. This might be the excuse the colonel at Fort Laramie needs to get them on to the reservation."

The mountain man paused a long moment, staring into space. Then he grunted and nodding to the sheriff, left the office.

* * *

Colonel Robert Weeks read the telegram again. He was a tall, thin, taciturn, officer, veteran of all the years of the Civil War. He had fought at Shiloh, Nashville and Chickamauga and had been with Sherman through the Georgia campaigns and back into the Carolinas.

After the surrender at Appomattox, Weeks, then a captain and a brevet lieutenant colonel, was assigned to units at Bismark, North Dakota, where the Seventh Cavalry had been sent to engage in quelling the Indians who had become rampant against the white settlers during the war years.

Once there, serving for several months, he had been assigned to the then new Fort Laramie, with the paramount duty of guarding the wagon trains coming through to California and protecting settlers in the area from Indian raids.

Promotions were slow if not non-existent and it was at a time when he was contemplating resigning his commission that he was promoted

to major and breveted colonel. With this incentive he stayed in uniform and gave himself to the task of bringing recalcitrant Indian chiefs to the reservation with their villages. It was a difficult task, for with summer coming on, entire villages left the winter areas where they had spent the 'Moons of White Skies'. They moved to grazing meadows and where they knew hunting should be good. With so many white-eyes coming, animals were rapidly disappearing from familiar hunting grounds, and the *Pte* were gone. Now and then a few buffalo might be found in some remote sector, but rarely.

Colonel Weeks sighed. He did not like forcing families from familiar terrain, where they and their ancestors had lived, hunted and fought for centuries. But the government favored the spread of the white settlers, Washington — the President — said to protect them, and to get the Indians on to the designated reservations. This

was his job, this he would do to the best of his ability.

"Sergeant O'Malley," he called through the open door of his office. In the next room the sergeant-major of the regiment assigned to Fort Laramie had his desk. A tall, heavy Irishman, with a furious orange-red moustache appeared in the doorway.

"Yes, sir?"

"Major Harris is out inspecting suds-row. Several of the men have been complaining the washwomen are not using enough soap and their uniforms are not coming out clean. But I need him here. Send a runner and have him come in."

Suds-row was back of the mess halls, where several local women did the washing and cleaning of uniforms and boots for the regiment. Paid a pittance and dependent upon tips from the soldiers and officers, the women were none too careful. It was an unwritten rule that any money found in pockets of the uniforms belonged to

the washer. Even so, the pay was poor and periodically the operation had to be inspected. This was where Major John Harris could be found at the moment.

He came through the door and looked at Colonel Weeks. "You wanted me?" he asked. The colonel waved him to a chair and spoke to the sergeant-major. "Come on in, Sergeant. What I have here will eventually involve you." Sergeant Timothy O'Malley, twenty-year veteran of the army, thanked him and took the only other vacant chair in the office.

Colonel Weeks handed the telegram to his executive officer and watched him read it. Reading it swiftly and then again more carefully, Major Harris handed it to the sergeant.

"This isn't some young bucks just out harassing settlers," Major Harris observed. "They've taken two white captives. They were after something more than just a momentary fling."

The colonel nodded. "Old Buffalo

116

Man has not refused to bring his village in to the reservation at Fort Robinson. But he has dragged his feet. I'm surprised that he would give us an excuse, such as this, to round him up and push him on his way."

"Excuse me, sir," the sergeant-major spoke up. He and the colonel had served together during the Sherman campaigns. Having found him at Fort Abraham Lincoln when he arrived and received his orders to Fort Laramie, the colonel had requested him as his top soldier. The noncommissioned officer felt free to enter into the conversation with the two officers.

"Sir, this *does* give you a good reason to get old Buffalo Man movin'. And there's the white man and woman — time is important in their case. Them young bucks are impatient and they just might use the captives to entertain the village before they move on to their summer range."

Colonel Weeks nodded. "We received a report from General Sheridan recently

advising us that now would be the opportune time to use some force in persuading recalcitrant chiefs to bring their villages into the reservations. The general has little patience with those of us," he grimaced wryly, "who have tried to be 'patient' with the savages."

"Yeah," commented the sergeant. "The only good Indian is a dead Indian, huh?"

"The general seems to have little regard for the actual welfare of our red brothers," Major Harris said dryly.

"Be that as it may," Colonel Weeks said, shrugging his shoulders in the heavy woollen jacket, "we have our orders to bring them into the reservations. And this present episode is hand-made for the reason to do our job. We'll do it, quickly and efficiently, and have old Buffalo Man and his tribe rounded up before they can say 'buffalo'."

"*Pte*," said the sergeant, grinning.

"Whatever," replied the commander, and with that the three of them settled

to serious planning for the swift, brief campaign they hoped to initiate.

★ ★ ★

The word of Bonner and Clara Somers' capture came to the Steele Horse Ranch two days following the incident. Steele was working a carefully chosen stallion to become his personal horse when Al Rooney returned from Red Bluff. Homer Bell, the huge mountain man, was sitting on a corral pole, watching him, and offering suggestions from time to time.

Leaning against the corral gate, Clint rolled a cigarette and listened to Rooney, his foreman. "Bell, here, was just telling me about it." He shook his head at the news. "I'm surprised Buffalo Man would let his young bucks put him in such a position," he said. He looked at Bell. "What do you think about it?"

Bell grunted and slid ponderously down from the top pole where he had

perched watching Clint's action with the stallion.

"It's that buck Cold Star," he said. "He's wanted to get his hands on Girl-With-Feet-Of-Deer ever since she begin to be a woman." His eyes grew cold and he looked at Steele.

"I'll need three hosses, gear, rifles and shells," he said softly and turning away walked toward the tackle shed and the corral where several horses were kept for immediate needs.

Clint nodded and followed by Al Rooney, he walked toward the corral. Taking a coil of lariat from a corral post, he entered the enclosure and built a loop.

9

COLONEL ROBERT WEEKS rose from his chair back of his desk and went to the window which overlooked the parade ground at Fort Laramie, Wyoming Territory. Two companies were forming, A and C, under the direction of Lieutenants Alfred Cross and Harry Long. Major Harris had asked to lead the companies in their task of moving Buffalo Man and his entire Cheyenne village from the mountain valley forty miles to the north-west, to Fort Robinson, an equal distance to the south and east.

Hands clasped behind him he watched the forming of the companies, hearing the calls of the sergeants, and watching the action of the horses lining up under the experienced hands of their riders.

400 men would attempt to move a village of a thousand occupants, men,

women and children, all reluctant to leave their valley. It would take two weeks, barring no accidents or incidents, to get them to the reservation. He sighed. He knew the wild nature of the young bucks, such as had attacked the stage at the Elk Mountain pass. They would be the ones who would stir up trouble with the move. He grimaced. Trouble or no trouble, it had to be done.

And aggravating the situation further was the fact that the village had to be searched for the two white captives, Bonner and the woman, Somers, carried away by those marauding young warriors. He shook his head. The army would be lucky to get this job done without losing some men, killed or wounded. And the Indians would fare no better.

He twisted his shoulders, irritatedly, in the heavy jacket and frowned. He was the one who should be leading this operation. But no, General Sheridan would not allow one of his rank

along on what the general termed 'a simple removal operation that should take no more than two companies and ambitious young lieutenants to lead them'. But, on the side of caution, without consulting Sheridan or his staff, the colonel was placing the action under the leadership of his second in command, Major John Harris. The general's staff would read the report, shrug their shoulders and probably never inform the general that a field rank was included in the operation.

"Corporal Johnson," he called to his striker, waiting in the next office, "inform Sergeant-Major O'Malley I am ready to review the troops."

The corporal appeared instantly in the doorway. "Yes, sir," he answered, and saluting, turned to make contact with the sergeant-major, waiting on the headquarters porch.

Straightening his blouse and donning his hat, the colonel stepped out. The two companies were drawn up before him on the parade ground,

riders standing by their horses, the lieutenants before their companies and Major Harris standing by to join the colonel in trooping the line.

Colonel Weeks nodded to Sergeant-Major O'Malley and they left the porch and advanced toward the major.

"*Companies . . . Attention!*" Major Harris's voice rolled across the parade ground. He faced the colonel, saluting.

"Companies A and C ready for inspection, sir," he informed the commanding officer. Colonel Weeks nodded.

"Very good, Major. Let's get this expedition on its way."

10

THE lodge where Bonner and Clara Somers were kept was on the outer perimeter of the village. The land was clear for fifty feet from the forest to the lodge. A few small bushes grew here and there, but the activity of the camp kept the ground mostly clear of growth of any kind.

The mountain man lay in concealment beside the slowly stiffening body of the village guard, whom he had killed. Hours passed and bluebottles found the dead Indian. Soon they were working the body until the exposed skin was covered by their buzzing presence. Bell paid little attention to it, until he saw a shadow slip across the ground before him.

He glanced up. He knew he had either to bury the body of the Indian,

or move away from it. Two buzzards were circling and others were coming in the distance. Soon a casual, graceful pattern of circling scavengers would announce to anyone within miles, that a dead body lay below. Someone would come to investigate what the buzzards had discovered.

Rising to a stooping position, he seized the body by the arms and dragged it back away from the perimeter of the forest. Once out of sight of the village, he lifted it in his arms and worked his way through several hundred yards of thicket and small lodge pines. He recalled a sharp defile with stones, seen as he came into the area.

Finding the defile, he rolled the body off the edge into the bottom of the depression and there placed it directly between two large boulders. Quickly he carried rock and brush and in a few minutes, had the body covered. The buzzards might circle, but it would be some time before the body would be discovered.

Back at the edge of the forest again, he saw that activity had picked up considerably. Breakfast fires were lighted, men and women were going from the lodges into the place of excrement and relieving themselves. Horses were being herded into flats closer to the camp where those to be used were being separated from the main body. Bell could see no great excitement among the people.

And he had discovered the lodge where the captives were being kept.

Standing before a lodge near the outer edge of the village was a young buck the mountain man had gambled with during his earlier visit to the camp of Buffalo Man. He remembered the young warrior's name, Fat Beaver. Beyond him the big mountain man studied the area, the lodge and the guard. He recalled that a mile from the village, well hidden in a thick copse of piñon and scrub pine, he had left the three horses borrowed from the Steele horse ranch. The

saddle-bags carried ammunition for three .44 calibre Winchester rifles, food for three days and each saddle-horn supported a full canteen of water.

If he could initiate the escape of Bonner and Clara Somers, he planned to lead them deep into the Wyoming canyon country. He hoped to escape the frantic search by Cold Star, certain to take place. Successful in evading the Indian, he would then guide them out of the mountains to wherever they might wish to go. Perhaps to some train watering point where they could continue their dash to give Sheridan, face to face, the information Clara Somer had for the army.

He glanced up at the sky. Two scavengers were gently circling above the rocky grave of the Cheyenne. But with the scent lowered by the burying, and the body out of sight, the scavengers were losing interest. If no curious buck noticed them and became interested in seeking out their

prey, he might be able to escape detection throughout the entire day, without having to shift his place of concealment.

He settled firmly in place, his eyes glued upon the lodge where he was certain his friends were captive. A plan was forming in his mind. It must be pitch dark, however, before he put the plan into action.

★ ★ ★

Todd Bonner was no coward: he did not worry about himself, but at the moment he was concerned about his situation and the woman with him. He was slowly working space between his wrists and the rope. If the Indian buck stayed out of the lodge for another hour, he would be free and could attack him when he arrived. One step at a time, he thought. Beyond overcoming the brave, (Cold Star, Clara had told Bonner his name), it would be playing it moment by moment.

The lodge entrance skins stirred and Cold Star stood before them. It was his second visit to the lodge since having Clara and Bonner secured there.

"My chief, Buffalo Man, is anxious to be away from this place with the sun tomorrow." He looked at Clara with glowering eyes and then turned to Bonner.

"We do not have time to chase you through the mountains like a maddened dog. You will be killed after you watch the woman burn."

Bonner met his gaze steadily. "Tell him what I say, Clara," said Bonner. Directing his words to the Indian, Bonner met his gaze unflinchingly.

"I am told you are called Cold Star," Clara interpreted, "I am called Bonner. I am a warrior as are you. I fought in the great war just ended among the white people. I killed many enemy. I will fight you for my life and for the woman."

Cold Star shook his head and grimaced. "Why should I fight you?

130

I have you captive. I can do with you as I will."

"I was told Cheyenne men would accept challenges. Why are you afraid to fight me? I have not been fed properly, I am hungry, my bones are tired from sitting one way for a long time. Yet you back away from me like a woman afraid of a yipping puppy." Clara cringed within herself, as she repeated Bonner's words. Since childhood she had known personally the furious anger of this Indian, almost maniacal. She expected to see Cold Star draw the knife from his sheath and kill Bonner where he lay, bound and helpless.

Cold Star flinched at the words. His face swelled with rage and his eyes blazed down at the bound white man. "You call me a woman?" he hissed, spittle spraying from his lips. His hand nearest the haft of his long-bladed skinning knife was clawed and trembled with his desire to draw it and slaughter this white man who had

the temerity to speak to him in such manner. His breath rushed through his nostrils until he snorted like an ox. His entire body jerked with his effort to control himself.

All this while Bonner lay seemingly relaxed, his eyes calmly fastened upon the face of the Indian brave. Slowly Cold Star fought for and gained control of his anger. He gave a gusty sigh and spoke, never taking his eyes from those of the white man.

"Tell this child of foolishness, who squawks like a bluejay in moulting season, that I will fight him, make him helpless, force him to watch you burn and then kill him as slowly and as painfully as possible. See if he can challenge this man with that knowledge before him!"

Clara's voice trembled as she interpreted the Indian's words to Bonner. "I'm frightened as I have never been frightened in my life," she whispered in closing.

"If it helps, I'm a little scared of

him myself," Bonner told her, with a grimace. He turned his attention to Cold Star.

"Then you agree, as a Cheyenne warrior, that if I fight you and win, I am to go free and take the woman with me?"

The grim-faced Indian stared at the white man. What can he do to me? thought the Indian. I am taller, younger and undoubtedly stronger. He is weakened for want of food and rest, and is older and not as agile as this man. Yes, I will vindicate the insults of this white-eye, destroy him and then his woman. Cold Star stared into the face of the white man, searching out a flicker of fear, but none came. He nodded.

"This man promises on his word as a warrior of The People, if you win in battle with me, you may go free and the woman with you. But only for four white man hours. We will fight at dark, and you will be dead before the early moon rides the skyroad."

Bonner nodded. "It is good," he said. He glanced at Clara. "Tell him it is only fair that I be fed now, and unbound so I may exercise my bones before destroying him before his tribe. Say that he must announce his promise before the fight begins, so there will be no capturing us before we have a chance to escape."

Clara interpreted Bonner's message and after a long minute of study, searching Bonner's face again with glowering eyes, Cold Star nodded. "It will be so."

He called the old woman up before him. Clara listened closely as he instructed the woman to prepare a full meal for the man and some more soup for the woman. They were to be freed from their bonds and allowed to exercise within the bounds of the lodge. They were not to be allowed outside the lodge, and guards would be placed about it.

When the door flap fell in place behind him, Clara quickly related to

Bonner what Cold Star had ordered. She called to the old woman who had crouched at one side of the tepee on her blankets, cringing as Cold Star confronted the captives.

"Mother," she said, her voice gentle, "you heard what the man Cold Star ordered. Make a large meal for the white man so he can gain strength. I will simply take some broth."

The old woman muttered and Clara asked her what she said. Working with a pot and some venison, preparing to cook the meal for Bonner, she answered Clara.

"This one said that Waken Tanka, The Grandfather Spirit, must honor you, for seldom has Cold Star changed his mind once he has decided what he will do. And to accept a challenge from a captive white man is strange, when all he has to do is kill him." The old woman shook her head, "strange," she muttered, "very strange."

"Perhaps Waken Tanka does not wish to have the blood of these white

people on the Cheyenne village," Clara said to her. "I am nothing, just a woman, but this man is a great man, a great warrior among his people, and has much land and cattle to the sun-rising place, near the Mother of Rivers. The Grandfather Spirit might be angry should he be harmed."

The old woman stared at her with blank eyes, and grunted.

★ ★ ★

Crouching beneath a low spreading pine, and surrounded with cedar and brush, the mountain man watched as Clara was taken to a post in the center of the open space. She was bound to the post, her arms pulled to the back and tied securely.

The people of the village were gathering. The word had gone out that Cold Star was fighting the white man and would kill him slowly so he might watch as the woman burned. Piled to one side of the space was a

heap of kindling and larger pieces of pine wood which would be piled at Clara's feet at the proper time.

Bonner was shoved to the center of the arena, his wrists unbound. Cold Star entered from the circle of the villagers and stood glaring at the white man.

"I will fight this white man and kill him," he said sonorously, his voice carrying over the area. "I will burn the white woman for her crimes against The People."

Bonner spoke, his voice equally loud. "Cold Star has promised that if I win the fight, I may take the white woman and leave, with four hours start, before anyone follows us."

Standing with members of his council, Buffalo Man stared at Cold Star. "Did you make this promise?"

Cold Star hesitated and then glaring at Bonner, nodded. "This man spoke such words," he said.

"Then so be it. I will see that the conditions are carried out," said

Buffalo Man. He gestured toward the center of the arena, now circled with hundreds of his people.

"Let this thing you have arranged," he said to Cold Star, "begin and be finished."

11

THE darling of Buffalo Man's lodge was his fourteen-year-old daughter, Moon Song. She was small, rounding in the early blessings of womanhood, shy and respectful of her elders. Already certain young men of the village had begun to take notice of her; Buffalo Man knew that one day soon suitors would begin to approach his lodge for more than his sage advice.

It was full dark. Moon Song could hear the noise of the villagers gathering at the sport field where she had been told the white woman, Girl-With-Feet-Of-Deer, was to be burned and Cold Star, the brash young warrior who had more than once smiled at her, was to fight the white man.

She left the chief's lodge to make a quick visit to the place for the women. Then she would go with an older sister

to watch the proceedings now taking the attention of the entire village.

As she entered the screen of trees that hid the place she sought from the eyes of the village, she was jerked up short by a powerful arm clasped about her neck. Before she could scream a huge hand clamped itself across her mouth. A hoarse voice whispered in her ear, speaking in Cheyenne.

"Moon Song, daughter of Buffalo Man, you know who I am. I will show myself in a moment. If you promise not to scream, I will turn you about so we can talk and you can see me. But if you scream, or call out, I will send you to the spirits without prayers and you will wander lost in the earth for an eternity. Do you understand?"

The girl was frightened and trembling. But she understood what was being said. To wander in the spirit world without purpose or hope, was unthinkable. Prayers for one dead must be uttered and the death dance made before the

spirit could go to the skies and be happy and live forever. She finally nodded her head vigorously.

Slowly, keeping his hand upon her mouth and his arm about her neck, Homer Bell turned the small girl until she could look him in the face. He saw recognition come into her eyes.

"Do you remember this man?" Bell spoke softly, his eyes holding hers in a stern gaze. She nodded again.

"You will not make a noise?" Her head shook negatively.

Slowly the hand over her mouth eased its grasp. "Moon Song, you will go with me, quietly and without words, to the far side of the place of sports where Cold Star is going to fight the white man. You will stay beside me without struggle." She nodded she understood.

With no further words the mountain man led her deeper into the fringe of the forest about the encampment, and silently moved with her around the circle until he found a place where he

could overlook the arena of the village. As he settled to watch the proceedings, he was about fifty feet from the center of the open space, where Clara was bound to the post.

★ ★ ★

Cold Star stepped from the circle of the chattering villagers, from the small grouping of the young braves who so often accompanied him on his raids, and approached to the center of the arena, facing Bonner.

He was stripped to the waist. Tall, an even six feet in height, his body tuned by exercise and stress of his forays against the whites, there seemed not an ounce of excess fat on his body. The light from fires, lighted about the circle, gleamed on his freshly greased torso, smeared by the knowing hands of his friends. His lower body was clad in a pair of buckskin pants, his feet encased in moccasins, laced to his calves. His hair was braided and

pulled back, held there by a leather headband.

Bonner faced him calmly. The white man was as tall, slightly heavier through the chest and with long arms and strong wrists. Seeing the Indian stripped to the waist, he pulled off his shirt. A murmur ran through the crowd as they saw the strongly muscled white body, hair down the center of the chest, and on one side, the blue, puckered scar of a bullet wound, reminiscence of his years of fighting in the Civil War. The sight of the wound brought knowledge that this man, too, was a warrior, and that Cold Star had a worthy adversary before him.

The Indian slowly and cautiously moved in on Bonner, his body taking the stance and making the movements of a wrestler. Bonner was aware that most Indians excelled in this sport, and spent much time from youth to adulthood in such competition. He, too, had wrestled much of his life, but never with an Indian. The grasps, the

holds, the throws would be somewhat different, but the basic principles were the same.

There was to be one other difference in this contest: it was to be to the finish: only one would walk away!

Bonner watched the approaching brave, calculating his moves against Cold Star; watching the eyes of his opponent, which would give away the moment of his attack. His body was relaxed, his hands out in front of him, ready for the moment Cold Star would launch into the battle. Bonner was determined the Indian must make the first move.

Cold Star did just that. Circling Bonner, he hissed through clenched teeth. "I will kill you, white man, and your scalp will hang from the ridge-pole of my lodge."

Bonner answered softly and calmly, his words carrying only to the Indian. "My adversary talks more than he fights. He must be an old woman, afraid to die."

He knew Cold Star did not know English and he had not understood what the Indian's words had been. But he knew the nature of the remark, from the look on Cold Star's face.

Cold Star launched the attack. Leaping high in the air, he threw himself at Bonner, his arms reaching, his feet kicking. Bonner moved lithely aside and the Indian skidded by him, swinging a long arm out in an attempt to throw him off balance. Bonner ducked the swing and kicked out, tripping Cold Star and sending him rolling in the dust.

Yelling in defiance, Cold Star came to his feet and again approached Bonner. This time he was set to grapple with him to achieve a wrestling hold and throw him to the ground. They met chest to chest. The same height, Bonner stared into the cold, killer eyes of the Indian.

Cold Star's body was greased, so it would be difficult for Bonner to hold him. As he closed with him,

145

Bonner grabbed the Indian's wrist and attempted to twist it back of him, for a pressure hold, but the greased arm simply twisted in his grasp. On the contrary, Cold Star seized Bonner's forearms in a firm grasp, and falling backwards, thrust with his feet, throwing the white man into the air and back over his head. Rolling as he hit the ground, Bonner was on his feet as quickly as the Indian and they closed upon each other again.

Neither could achieve an advantage hold over the other. Both strained and grunted, digging in with their feet and pushing, straining in an attempt to throw the other off balance. The muscles of their arms and shoulders bulged with their efforts, and the dust of the arena rose about them as they struggled, two men from vastly different cultures, each trying to conquer the other, each knowing that the loser would either be dead or die.

Suddenly Bonner, straining forward

with all his might, quickly reversed himself and fell backwards and to the side. Holding tightly to the Indian's forearms, he tossed Cold Star over his head and leaping to his feet, as the brave came to his feet, kicked him solidly in the face. The Indian grunted and fell back, recovering and once again leaping to the attack.

Coming at Bonner he feinted and the white man, maneuvering to the Indian's movements, found himself falling backwards, his feet kicked from under him. He rolled and dodged Cold Star, who had leaped with both feet at his stomach, attempting to drive his heels deep into Bonner's middle.

Reaching out with his long arms, the Indian attempted to bring Bonner into a bear-hug, but the white man seized an arm, ducked under it, and twisting, threw the brave for a hard fall over his hip upon the ground. Stunned, Cold Star shook his head. "Ah" and "ooo" sounds went through the crowd. Very

seldom had they ever seen Cold Star thrown so hard.

Taking advantage of the Indian's momentary stun, Bonner launched himself bodily at Cold Star. The Indian rolled aside and Bonner struck the ground and grunted with the hard pounding his body took in the fall. A savage kick took him in one side, and another to the kidney area, and then, shooting with pain, he found his footing and met the Indian in a chest to chest hold again.

Watching from his place of conceal-ment, Homer Bell knew that eventually the Indian would get the best of Bonner. If Cold Star felt he was losing the fight, he might signal a friend to toss him a war-club, or a hatchet or even a knife. The Indian would fight fair only so long as he felt he was winning.

The mountain man held Moon Song with a hand over her mouth and an arm about her shoulders. His grasp was gentle, but she knew it could tighten drastically in a moment. The

young girl was frightened and watched the fight before her with widened, fearful eyes. She could not think what part she might play in all that was transpiring before her, but she sensed this huge white man, holding her captive, although gentle with her, could suddenly become very violent. She remained silent and still.

Bonner was beginning to tire. He was aware that his opponent was younger than he, more wiry, and more accustomed to this type of fighting. It was without thinking that Bonner instinctively and suddenly changed his defence.

As Cold Star threw himself at the white man again, Bonner suddenly moved away from him and brought up his hands, clenched into fists. This made no impression upon the Indian. It was just another white-man way of fighting, clumsy and ineffective.

Homer Bell noticed and nodded grimly. Indians had not yet learned the white man's use of the fist as a

weapon. The art of boxing had not yet entered their repertory of conflict. The fist was not used as a means of offensive fighting.

Bonner had learned the rudiments of boxing while in the army during the Civil War. A sergeant from New York City had been the champion of his company. As a friend to Bonner, he had shown him the movements, the defences and the blows, and impressed upon him the importance of moving opposite the opponent's seemingly natural movement.

Cold Star seemed to be moving to his left when he circled Bonner. accordingly, remembering the instructions of the sergeant, Bonner moved to his left, causing the Indian to break stride and move from his natural stance. As he did so Bonner moved into him and struck with his left fist, sinking it into Cold Star's stomach.

The brave grunted and glared at the white man. This was unexpected and new to him. Overcoming his

momentary loss of breath, Cold Star rushed directly at Bonner, who was expecting such a movement.

The white man whipped aside, and as the Indian whirled past, he sank a straight right-hand blow into the kidney area of the brave. Cold Star yelled in pain and fury. He whirled and leaped at Bonner, striving to use his feet against the fists, but the white man dodged and as the Indian found his footing and turned, Bonner was there.

A left fist hooked to the stomach again, and as the Indian bent forward briefly, the right fist, with all the power and weight of Bonner back of it, met Cold Star's narrow jaw. The Indian staggered and wavered on his feet. He shook his head and stood momentarily dazed.

A roar went up from the crowd. Their champion was not winning. The white man was using some sort of magic with his hands.

A brave slipped to the edge of the crowd and called to Cold Star. "Here,

brother, use this and kill the white-eye! Do not let him disgrace you before your village!" A steel-bladed hatchet whirled through the air and landed at the feet of Cold Star. Quickly recovering from his daze, and yelling in defiance, the Indian stooped and seizing the weapon, made a headlong dive at Bonner.

A gun roared! The crowd surged back from the edge of the circle, as Cold Star stopped his lunge and fell back, sprawling unconscious, blood dripping from his head.

"Bonner! Grab that axe! Cut Clara loose!"

Homer Bell advanced into the area, the smoking gun in one hand, and his arm squeezing about the neck of Moon Song. He faced Buffalo Man and met the old man's astonished stare.

"Buffalo Man," Bell said in the language of The People, "I have your daughter's life in my hands." He placed the barrel of the cocked six-gun to Moon Song's temple. "It is up to you

whether she lives or dies."

"If she dies, you will die with her, white man!" said the chief, his eyes now darting hate at the mountain man.

"True, but before I die, your daughter, your wife and you will fall from my bullets. That is not necessary. My white friend has released the woman you would burn. We will leave, taking Moon Song with us for one hour. We will release her, but you will wait one more hour before you start looking for her and following us. We will be far away and you will not find us."

"You are foolish, White Man of the Mountains. One of my warriors is aiming his rifle at your head this moment. He shoots and my daughter is free — "

"He shoots and my cocked gun explodes her head into your lap, old man," Bell said softly, and the chief believed him. Buffalo Man gestured to the brave levering the rifle at the mountain man, and the Indian

153

lowered the weapon, mouthing threats and grunting his frustration.

"Old man," said Homer Bell loudly, so all could hear, "my friend has cut the woman loose and we are leaving." Then he ran a bluff, hoping it would work. "A Crow army scout friend is watching the village for us. If anyone leaves the village to follow us he will signal me and your daughter, although I do not want to do it, will die. We leave now."

Holding the gun to the girl's temple, he whispered to her. "I will not harm you. Do not struggle." He backed away with her, and for the first time saw that Bonner and Clara were just to one side of him, moving as he moved. He nodded at the inert body of Cold Star.

"Is he dead?" he whispered hoarsely to Bonner from one corner of his mouth.

"You usually hit what you shoot at don't you?" Bonner said. "He looks dead to me."

The three white people and the Indian girl backed slowly into the darkness of the forest encircling the arena. Homer Bell heard the voice of Buffalo Man.

"Let no one leave the village," the old chief shouted. "If anyone does, and my daughter dies because of your leaving, that one will die at the stake in the white woman's place!"

"Do you have a Crow scout watching?" asked Bonner, as they moved quickly away from the village.

"Nope," said Bell, "but they don't know it!"

12

HOMER BELL led Bonner and Clara on a circuitous route, away from the Elk Mountain stronghold of Buffalo Man. His trail was his own, cut through forests, down sharp gorges and up steep inclines. The route he took did not at any time make contact with any travelers, nor did they find it necessary to hide from Buffalo Man's warriors, by this time seeking them. Moon Song had been released, as Bell had promised, an hour out of the Indian camp. By now she had undoubtedly been found and was back safe with her family.

At high noon they paused beneath a looming mesa overhang and ate from their meagre food supply, brought in saddle-bags by the mountain man. Bell stood looking into the distance back along the way they had come.

"We are being followed, without doubt," he said to them. "That old Injun ain't gonna give up until he tracks us down."

He turned and searching the distance, raised a hand and pointed. "Over thar is whar we are goin'," he said, pointing. "The Steele ranch where I got these hosses is under that roll of hills over thar. But we ain't goin' thar. We foller the mesa here, an' just north of Fort Laramie we hit the Black Hills trail. It's been thar fer hundreds of years."

"An Indian trail?" asked Bonner.

"In the beginnin', I reckon. The Cheyenne say their forefathers, The Old Ones, they call 'em, made the trail originally. It leads to the Black Hills, which are sacred to Sioux and Cheyenne. Wagoners use it now, frum Fort Laramie to Custer City. We'll foller it to Custer City. You can get a stage thar to Fort Abraham Lincoln, where you're headin' for."

Clara sighed. Finally they were on their way to confront General Sheridan

157

and tell him what she had heard about the plains tribes gathering into a huge force. And . . . finally, she was out of the reach of Cold Star.

She recalled with a shudder the Cheyenne brave lying in the dust before the post where she was bound. His splendid body was lax in the unattractive sprawl of death, blood surrounding his black head.

Cold Star would no longer be the destroyer of her happiness or bring her dark terror in the deeps of the night. She would find safety among her own kind. How far away they were, she thought. Indiana, a small green spot far beyond the Mississippi River; how would she ever manage to get there, with no money, no companion to side her? She shook her head. That was still in the future. Right now, she had to get off this mesa, relying upon these two men for each step she took.

★ ★ ★

It was a grueling experience. Even for Bonner, range-hardened and strong as he was, the days were tiring. He wondered about the woman, how she could stand the long hours of the rough trail, the constant pitch and movement of the horses as they worked their up the sides of ravines, down impossible slopes and through icy streams.

She did not complain. Exhausted when they came to time for camp, she nevertheless slid from the saddle, tended to her horse and began the chore of making a fire and aiding in preparing for the evening meal. If there was a nearby stream, she would bathe, and wrapped in a blanket, take her place near the fire and soon was deep in slumber. She had declared to herself, she was no longer Girl-With-Feet-Of-Deer. She was Clara Somers, white woman, going back to her people. If they would not have her, she would make her own way.

But as she lay there during those nights of camping along the dark trail,

she wondered about Todd Bonner. He had not talked about himself. He was quiet, almost sombre. Bell was lost in his reminiscences. Now and then he would talk about mountain rendezvous he had attended when mountain men and Indian tribes would meet for relaxation and trading, enjoying themselves after long months of trapping the streams of the mountains and valleys.

One evening Bell, following what had been long hours traveling across difficult terrain, brought them up-to-date as to their location on their journey.

"Thar's a way-station about one day's journey frum here," he told them as they pulled up to make camp. It was a small protected pocket, facing a fast-falling stream. There was spring forage for the horses, and the water came cold and clear from the hills about them.

"We kin rest thar fer a day or so, get you restocked an' you kin be on yore way again," he continued. Clara paused

in what she was doing and looked over to where he was building the fire for the evening meal.

"You said *you* instead of *we*, Homer. Aren't you going on with us to Fort Abraham Lincoln?"

Bonner, unsaddling his horse and placing the gear and blankets closer to the fire, straightened and stood listening for the mountain man's reply.

Bell struck a match and held it to the pine slivers and dried moss he had gathered for tinder. As the tiny blue flame grew and brightened, he added more small fuel, until a substantial blaze was licking upward.

He shook his head. "Nope, Miss Clara. I ain't goin' any further with you. It's a clear way an' over at the Cheyenne River Agency thar's a military post. Frum thar you can go by stage right into Fort Abraham Lincoln. You won't need me no longer."

Bonner came over to stand beside Clara. "You've been more than generous with your time, Homer, in coming this

161

far with us. We appreciate it. And you feel we will be safe to Custer City on to the Cheyenne River Agency? No roving Indian bands to try for our hair?"

Homer Bell shook his head. "Any bands goin' through this area are way off th' reservation an' ain't hankerin' to call attention to theirselves. Old Sittin' Bull has put out th' call, all right, an' they are goin' to him."

As they sat eating the fried venison and the last potatoes in their bag of provisions, the mountain man enlarged upon the fact of the Indians leaving the reservations.

"Injun agents ain't reportin' their goin'," he said.

"Why, that's wrong," Clara said. "White families, travelers or just people like us are in danger. Surely the agents are reporting the movement to the army, at least?"

The mountain man shook his head. "Nope. If they reported it to the army, the army would report it to Washington an' a investigation would be made.

They'd find that th' agents has been falsifyin' reports, sayin' th' head count's the same, so the same amount of supplies for the Injuns would keep on comin'. With the Injuns not there to use the supplies, blankets, food, beeves, the agents are gettin' rich sellin' th' goods an' keepin' th' money. They ain't about to report short head counts to th' agency boss in Washington City. It'd put a crimp to their own personal gold mine, an' maybe even get some of 'em fired from their jobs."

Bonner shook his head. "That just isn't right," he said. He looked at Clara. "That may be the very reason General Sheridan was reluctant to accept your report about a large gathering. The agents' reports of normal population is relayed to General Sherman, who is in charge of all army activities in Washington, and then on to General Sheridan, who is heading up the operation to bring a peaceful solution among the Indians and whites here in the West."

Homer Bell mouthed a piece of venison and chewed thoughtfully. "I reckon yo're right," he said. "An' that's why it should be purty safe fer you'ns to go on by yourselves to Custer City."

★ ★ ★

The way-station was set in a small flat facing a pond formed by water coming out of the rolling hills back of it. There were corrals with several horses, and a rack with a half-dozen saddled horses standing hip-shot before it. All this Bonner saw when the three rode up before the low-beamed structure that was the main cabin.

It did not take long to learn that the stage was not running through to Custer City. Too many quick raids by small bands of roaming Indians, with several drivers and passengers killed and some captured and carried away, had brought a stop to the service.

Homer Bell helped in resupplying their provisions and told them farewell.

Bonner and Clara rested themselves and their horses for two days following the mountain man's departure, and then again set out upon the trail leading to the Cheyenne River Agency at Fort Sully.

13

GENERAL Philip Sheridan stood at the window of his office, looking out over the parade ground of Fort Abraham Lincoln. He watched a segment of the 7th Cavalry drilling, the fog-horn voice of the drill sergeant coming muted through the walls of the room. Seated in a chair beyond his desk was Lieutenant Colonel George Armstrong Custer, his small-set, bright blue eyes centered upon blue smoke rings rising from a strong-scented cigar held in one hand.

"The troops look good, Custer," the gravelly voice of his commander reached him. "They look strong and ready for whatever this summer brings."

"They're ready, General," the rather high-pitched tones of Custer answered. "The finest group of men, in the best

regiment of fighting men in the world, sir," he added.

"Hummph," the general grunted, still eyeing the troops. "They tell me that the Comanche brave, mounted upon his well-trained war-pony, clad in breech-cloth and moccasins, armed with lance and shield, is even yet the better warrior, man for man."

Custer laughed, throwing back his recently barbered blond head, the hair shorter than he usually wore it. "He's good, no doubt about it, General. Very good. But armed as we are, the buck on his pony won't stand a chance against my men, on army, battle-trained horses, and armed with our repeating rifles and sixshot hand-guns."

The general turned back to his desk and sat, leaning back and looking at Custer. He took a cigar from a humidor on the desk and lit the black cylinder, blowing a stream of smoke toward the ceiling.

"I received two reports this week,"

the short, brusque general said, his black eyes penetrating as they bored into the face of his younger counterpart. "One was disturbing; one was rather satisfying." He puffed on his cigar and studied Custer's expression.

"Scouts brought in various reports of Indians leaving the reservations in droves. Yet the reports from agents on the different reservations indicate no loss in head count, no movement of Indian families or groups of braves. Other scouting news is that there is a gathering, a growing crowd, many complete villages from the reports, over along the Rosebud."

Custer, his yellowish moustache drooping over his rather feminine mouth, returned the general's stare and remained silent, puffing on his own cigar. The blue haze drifted to the ceiling as the general continued.

"That was the disturbing news. The other is that Colonel Robert Weeks, over at Laramie, has rounded up old Buffalo Man of the Cheyenne and

finally got him on to the reservation at Fort Robertson. He said that during the trip nearly fifty of the younger warriors slipped away into the mountains. But the village, with their chief, is finally on the reservation."

"Those bucks heard Sitting Bull's call early in the winter," Custer said. "He apparently wants to get as many as possible together and try to live the old ways again. Those young braves have gone to join up with him." He was silent for a moment and then continued.

"Sitting Bull's call don't bother me so much," he said quietly, "it's that damn mystic, Crazy Horse and his Oglalas. You can never tell which way he's going to jump. And he's one to stir up a bunch of troublemakers. And they'll follow him, for they think he's the reincarnation of ancient medicine men."

Sheridan nodded. "We're gonna have our hands full this summer." He stirred and brought his sharp gaze back to

Custer's face. "Have the Seventh ready to go at any time. We may be taking the trail sooner than expected or planned."

Custer sat forward in his chair, knocking ashes from his cigar into a flat, chipped tray on the general's desk, used for that purpose. "The Seventh can take half its men and ride through whatever Sitting Bull has planned, all the Indians he wants to bunch together, and back again. We'll be ready, in fact, we are ready. We could ride out tomorrow if the general said the word!" The bright blue eyes clashed with the dark, piercing orbs of the general.

General Sheridan nodded. He knew the youngest general of the Civil War believed what he was saying, even if purer knowledge spoke of its improbability.

★ ★ ★

Fort Sully was a small military post near the Cheyenne River Indian Agency,

consisting of two companies of troops, sutler, the tack barn, and corrals for the horses, all surrounded by a stockade of pine and aspen logs hauled from the surrounding hills.

A well had been dug inside the stockade, near the enlisted troops' mess hall. The post was simply there to make a statement to the Indians controlled by the agency. The United States Army was present to protect the citizens passing through, and to give assurance of strength and determination.

Being only two companies, and neither at full strength, the efficiency of the force was questionable. The determination of achievement of purpose depended upon the willingness of the troopers to follow their leaders. As so often happened, the far outposts of the military structure in the West received only the officers with the poorest efficiency ratings. Quite often the running of the establishment rested upon the experience and the value of the senior non-commissioned soldiers,

the sergeants. These factors, heightened by the loneliness of a far-flung outpost, created a low morale among the soldiers assigned there.

Between the post main gates and the river, were several lodges of families of Indians, who were allowed to reside near the post. They were employed in various ways about the installation, and in certain lodges were the families of Ute and Crow scouts for the two companies based there.

Each company was commanded by a senior lieutenant. Captain William Bellows was the post commander and in charge of the activities of the companies.

It was mid-afternoon when Todd Bonner and Clara Somers rode up to the main gate and were stopped by the gate guard.

"We would like to see your commanding officer," Bonner said. The guard was eyeing Clara curiously. A woman dressed in male pants, wearing a thigh-length Indian braided jacket, with

a wide-brimmed hat thrust on her head, certainly stirred his interest. The fact that she was of female gender beneath the male attire was obvious, however. Clara, warm in the late June sun, had opened her jacket and the fullness of her bosom left no doubt as to her sex.

"Corporal of the Guard," the soldier stepped to the gate sally-port and bawled at the top of his voice. "Post number one, on the double!"

A curious crowd of Indian onlookers began to gather about them. The women eyed Clara and gabbled among themselves. Clara wondered what they would do if they knew she understood most of what they were saying. The Ute and Cheyenne tongues were closely related, many of the words the same. Crow intonation and guttural inflections were harder, but here and there she understood a phrase.

Bonner glanced at her. "Do you know what they are talking about?"

She nodded. "That we are strangers, and that we are traveling together,

then we must be blanket mates." She smiled. "Indian women are very earthy and their minds run to the simple and . . . essential things."

He grinned and nodded. "I can understand that," he said. Before he could continue, the corporal of the guard emerged from the sally-port and approached them

You wished to see the commanding officer?" he asked, his keen eyes taking in the travel-worn gear, the sturdy horses and the apparently experienced travelers.

"If we may," said Bonner. "Why are your gates barred and guarded? I thought most posts admitted travelers without question — white travelers."

The corporal shrugged. "There's been orders to tighten up security," he said. He turned to the guard. "Let them in. I'll let Captain Bellows know they are here." He touched the brim of his hat to Clara and, giving a brief salute to Bonner, entered the stockade again. "There must be some movement afoot

among the tribes," Bonner murmured to Clara. She glanced at him and then, leaning over, spoke softly to the nearest Indian woman.

"Sister, why is the white man's place here guarded with guns and gates with bars across? Is there not peace between the white man and our people?"

The Indian woman looked at her. "You say our *people*, yet I see white skin simply touched by the sun, not by birth."

"I was raised in the lodge of a Cheyenne sub-chief," Clara said. "This white man freed me from Buffalo Man's village and is returning me to my people beyond the Father of Waters."

The woman eyed her and then nodded. "There is trouble," she said softly. "Our young men are angry with the white man who runs the agency. The Grandfather in Wash-ing-town sends much beef to the reservation to be given us for food. But we get very little. The men cannot hunt for there are no deer or buffalo on the

reservation. They say the men must plant seeds and eat what grows. But what can we eat while it is growing?"

"One must eat," Clara said gently. "Where are your young men? Are they the ones causing trouble?"

The woman nodded and looked about her nervously. Other women and some of the men were watching her closely. "They are causing trouble along the trail from here to the town of Bismark where the leader of the blue coats lives. The one with the yellow hair is there. This place is afraid the young men will attack here."

"Will they attack here?" asked Clara. The woman was edging away. She was being watched and mutterings were rising among the Indians.

"Maybe," she whispered and turning, she walked back among the women and children and disappeared into the crowd.

"Y'all can come on in." The corporal of the guard had reappeared. The soldier nodded to the gate guard. "Let

'em through," he said.

The gate opened and then closed quickly behind them. The corporal led them across a dusty compound into a row of buildings, one with a hand-painted sign in white letters, indicating it was *Headquarters*. A burly officer, bare-headed and with a cigar in one hand, waited on the porch of the central building.

Bonner and Clara pulled their mounts to the hitch-rail before the headquarters and dismounted. The corporal mounted the steps and saluted the officer.

"Captain Bellows, sir, this here is a Mr Bonner and a Miss Somers. They just come off the Cheyenne River trail."

Captain Bellows held out his hand. "Welcome to Fort Sully," he said as they shook hands. He nodded to Clara and smiled. "Welcome, Miss Somers. Both you come on in out of the sun. You must be tired. That's a rough trail."

He turned and led them into the

building. A private soldier, working on a report of some kind, started to rise but the captain waved him down. "Carry on, Meadows," he said. "I'm going to visit with these folks for awhile. Maybe you might scare up some coffee and donuts for us, eh?"

"Yes, sir." The young soldier rose and taking his hat hurried from the room.

"The mess sergeant has a light touch with donuts," the captain said, conversationally, as they entered his office. "That is rare around here, and even in the army. They are usually hard enough to shoe horses with."

Bonner grinned. "I've eaten those kind, too," he said. The captain waved to chairs in front of his desk and then seated himself back of it.

They chatted for a short while. Bonner explained Clara's presence and that they had been over the Black Hills road and then the Cheyenne River trail to get them where they were.

"And what can I do, or what can the

army do for you, Mr Bonner?" Captain Bellows asked.

"We need to get to Fort Abraham Lincoln the swiftest way possible," Bonner said. "Miss Somers has information that General Sheridan wishes to hear face to face. He would not accept telegraphed explanations of what she knows and thinks he should know."

Bellows looked at Clara closely. "Do you think you can trust me with that information?" he asked, with a smile.

Bonner looked at her and shrugged. "I can't see where it would matter much," he told her.

Speaking slowly and watching the captain's face as she did so, Clara related what she knew about Sitting Bull's call for the tribes to leave reservations and gather with him at a place the Indians called The Valley of the Greasy Grass. She also pointed out that when she escaped Buffalo Man's village, he was at the point of taking his village out of Elk Mountains and

traveling to join Sitting Bull at the appointed place.

"Well, Buffalo Man didn't get his way," Bellows told them. "I got word this week that before he could get his village away, the army from Fort Laramie arrived and shooed them into the reservation at Fort Robinson."

"Young men and all?" asked Clara.

Bellows shook his head. "No. According to reports some fifty bucks got away from the village *en route*; most of them were young men." He sighed. "We've been having some trouble around here with much the same problem. Bucks jumping the reservation and raiding and rioting, killing settlers and miners, then slipping back on the grounds and denying ever being away."

"Do you think some of Buffalo Man's braves are among those making the trouble?" asked Bonner. "That's a pretty far piece for them to travel just to raise some ruckus."

The captain looked at him and

grimaced. "You're here, aren't you? It is a far piece, yes, but you made it. They could also, if they got wind that others in this area were rousting the white-eyes, especially the army."

Bonner nodded. "Captain, like I said, we need to get to Fort Abraham Lincoln. What do you suggest?"

The captain rose and walked to a window overlooking the parade ground. He turned, his face sad. He shook his head.

"My friends, you are a week too late. Custer left Fort Abraham Lincoln with the Seventh Cavalry to join General Crook at the Little Rosebud Creek. Instead he ended up at the Little Big Horn, in the middle of a battle with about three thousand Indians all Sioux, or friends or relatives of the Sioux. July 25th, he was killed. Killed along with two hundred and twenty-seven men, an entire company." He was silent, his face lined, his eyes distant. "Custer, his brother Tom and

a nephew were all killed. Most were scalped." He paused and then said in almost a whisper, "Yellow Hair was not scalped. They honored him too much as a warrior to do so."

14

SITTING BULL. Scorned by the whites because of his name, yet holding, in the mind of the tribes, the most honored name of all, for the buffalo bull, powerful and wise, whose entire body could be used for life itself, was the most honored of all creatures of the plains.

He was a mystic. It was said he talked with all animals and understood them, but he understood the *Pte* most of all. Unlike most mystics, however, he was not remote or unapproachable or feared. Instead he loved his people, walked among them and was touched by them. He lifted the children in his arms and their mothers felt their little ones were then doubly blessed.

Early a celebrated warrior, coups made too numerous for counting, only for recounting at tribal functions, he

was now looked upon as the leader among The People. So his call went out and hearing it were Hunkpapas, his own tribe, Oglalas, Blackfeet, Sans Arcs, Miniconjoux, Bannocks and Cheyenne. And they come to the place called by The People 'Greasy Grass', by a river named by white surveyors, Little Big Horn.

It was here Sitting Bull had his great vision. After twenty-four hours of fasting and searching the minds of those speaking from the shadows, he called his council.

He sat in his temporary tepee, deep in the center of the largest encampment ever assembled by and for The People. "Come to me," he had called them by his news riders. "Come and we will live the way of our fathers, the old way. We will follow the *Pte* and live on the breast of Grandmother Earth. We will rid our world of the blue-coat soldiers and never again will we go hungry."

They were seated around the council fire. The heat was oppressive, but none

gave indication of being uncomfortable. Sitting Bull sat at the peak of the circle. To his right sat Crazy Horse, his war chief, a mystic himself, chief of the Oglalas, but a renowned warrior having a great following among his people. To his left was Red Cloud, lesser chief of the Oglalas, but a warrior of great fame, and known for many coups and unusual bravery in the face of the enemy.

The chests of these three leaders of The People showed the scars from the ancient Sun Dance, badges of courage and determination under great pain and duress. Hours of leaning against the leather and wooden pins thrust through the flaps of flesh on the chest, staring into the sun, chanting every moment, until the spirits released them into oblivion.

The circle was completed by lesser chiefs and war chiefs. They watched the great prophet and holy man, now in his middle forties. His eyes were slitted, staring into the fire. All remained silent.

The great one was communing with the spirits of the fire.

He stirred and gestured to a young brave standing back of him. Quickly, but reverently, a pipe, fully tamped with tobacco, was handed him. He leaned forward and taking a twig from a selected pile, got it drawing. He made the reverent gestures to the four places of the wind, and handed the pipe to Crazy Horse, sitting to his right.

Crazy Horse repeated the gestures and the pipe then continued around the circle. Emptied once, it was replenished and continued to pass around the council circle until it was back to Sitting Bull. He carefully tapped the ashes reverently into the fire, and handed the instrument to the young warrior waiting to receive it.

"I have had a vision," he said in his soft, rumbling voice, a voice that held those listening enthralled at its resonance, and the words which often conjured up visions within their minds.

"I have had a vision," he repeated.

"There will be a great battle. The blue coats will fall from the hills as rain falls from the clouds. They will attack again and again; some of our bravest will go to those hunting lands beyond the sky. Old men and women and children must immediately go into the hills and wadis to hide and be safe. Warriors must put on their most sacred paint, prepare their finest weapons and horses. It will be a battle long remembered by both the white-eyes and The People alike."

He was silent a long time. There was very little stirring among those waiting his final words. When they came, there was a great sigh of wonder and pleasure around the circle.

"The People will win the battle," he said strongly, his obsidian eyes wide and glittering. "Among the blue coats to die will be the one called Long Hair or Yellow Hair. I must now warn each of you and you must warn all your braves: anyone killing Long Hair, or seeing him lying dead or wounded, may count coup only on him. He

must not be mutilated or spat upon. He is among the greatest of soldiers of the white man. He is honored by the White Grandfather in Wash-ing-town. We will honor him in his death by not disturbing him, so his spirit will be free to go to its far place in the sky." He looked about the circle. There were short nods of agreement and a grunt or two. Not all of them held the yellow-haired leader of the Seventh Cavalry in such awe. However, most would give a fine horse or even a favorite woman to count coup upon his body, much less take the hair and hang it from his lodge pole.

"Go now," Sitting Bull intoned. "Prepare. Tomorrow you will fight the white man. We will conquer and will live as did our fathers and their fathers before them. We will go back to the old ways and follow the *Pte* and be prosperous and happy once more."

Once the council was gone, Sitting Bull's youngest wife, just past sixteen, brought him a gourd of herb tea which

he loved, and his first wife handed him a bowl of stew. He ate and drank slowly and thoughtfully.

Long Hair . . . Yellow Hair . . . *Custer* was his white-man name. He was indeed a great warrior and would bring the white soldiers swarming. Knowing they were coming, alerted by his scouts. Crazy Horse assured Sitting Bull that his warriors would destroy every white soldier crossing the Little Big Horn River, or touching one inch of the hills about it.

He shrugged his shoulders and grunted. Maybe. But the outcome was foresworn. 12,000 braves, stripped for battle, eager to kill the white soldiers, eager to find the old ways and no longer be hunted down and forced on to reservations where they were not allowed to hunt, where food was scarce and they watched their wives and children grow weak and thin.

It was strange; he shook his head. Long Hair, of all men of war, should know that his forces could not stand

against the might of the warriors gathered against him . . .

★ ★ ★

"It is time to go, old man," wife number one came and touched his shoulder.

He sighed. Yes, indeed it was time to go. It was over. The blue coats had come. They had fallen as snowflakes from the skies, down the brows of the hills, across the river, into the encampment.

Throughout the long, bloody day they had fought. Finally, his head bared and gleaming in the sun, wounded, Long Hair had led his soldiers, over 200 of them, up the slope beyond the river. Pursued by 3,000 warriors, screaming and brandishing clubs, spears, firing ancient muskets and a few newer weapons, releasing arrow after arrow until a forest of them cascaded through the air, they fought! The companies of the Seventh Cavalry were encircled

and killed. Every man. Every horse, save one, the white one ridden by Long Hair.

Quietness came upon the slope then a hum rose, voices low and in awe, the sound of a thousand bees in excitement. The one with the Yellow Hair had fallen. And now he had died! Gallantly, fighting to the last bullet and breath! He fell and his men fell beside him, until the long wind whispered in silence across the slopes of Greasy Grass.

The warriors followed Sitting Bull's orders: Long Hair was not touched. He lay there, his blue eyes staring into the hot sky, his men scattered in grotesque shapes about him, his revolver falling from pale, limp fingers.

Sitting Bull sat in his lodge, temporarily erected, hurriedly so, because the women knew that after this battle the whites would come in swarms. They would have quickly to repack their lodges and leave Greasy Grass forever.

The mystic received the report of the

battle from his friend and companion, Crazy Horse. "They came, as you visioned," said the warrior chief, his small eyes gleaming in pleasure. "They were like rain falling from the sky. We met them and drove them across the river. We killed them like squirrels from the trees, or turkeys in the bushes. They fought, but were unable to escape us. Long Hair fell! We have defeated the white-eyes!"

★ ★ ★

. . . And the young Cheyenne woman, Monaseata, went to the hill and sat beside the body of Long Hair. She cut herself and bleeding, sang the songs of death to help his spirit along to the place in the sky. Long Hair's son, gotten from their love and her body, sat beside her and looked at the dead man.

And wondered why his mother wept and sang . . .

15

CLARA was taken to the quarters of the captain, where an elderly woman, wife of a deceased soldier, was a live-in housekeeper. She was given a cot in the woman's bedroom, and spent the afternoon resting and talking over coffee and a plate of freshly baked sugar cookies.

Bonner took his bedroll to the livery and there, in a corner, cushioned by prairie hay scattered on the floor, he spread his tarp and blankets. Later on he strolled to the sutler's store and bar.

Sipping a glass of raw liquor, he leaned on his elbows and watched a poker game. Two civilians and two soldiers were engaged in trying to outguess the dealer and each other, over pots never reaching more than five dollars. It was nearing the end of

June and the first of the month payrolls had long since disappeared.

The sutler tended bar and worked over a dog-eared log as he did so. He spoke to Bonner.

"Just come in?" he asked.

"Yes." Bonner said, handing him his glass for a refill.

"I guess you're not stayin'. There sure ain't much here."

Bonner sipped his second drink, savoring the raw, biting taste after the long days on the trail. He did not answer the sutler. One of the men playing cards looked over at him and eyed him carefully. Finally he folded his cards and pushed back from the table. He thumbed his hat back on his tousled head and spoke to Bonner.

"Th' story is that you brung a right purty squaw into th' post. That right?"

Bonner continued to sip his drink, leaning back on the bar, and still did not answer.

"Word is that she's at least half white and about as purty as a picture.

194

Nice figure of a woman, too. She yore woman?"

Bonner continued to eye the man carefully. There was something about the man's face that betrayed the fact he was a gunman. As he pushed back his chair and stood, Bonner could see the tied-down end of his holster.

"I think I know you," the man said. "I've heard about someone over there in the Dakotas that wuz related to that old outlaw, John Wesley Hardin. An' his name wuz Bonner. Would that be you?"

"Now, Rufe, you just settle down an' let it alone," the sutler said. "The camp commander done told me there's too much rough stuff goin' on around my store. Now, you cool it."

"You stay out of this, Morgan." Rufe glared at the sutler. "This here is between me an' that rannie." He looked at Bonner. "I ast you a question."

Bonner sat his glass on the bar; he placed a coin beside the glass and spoke to the sutler.

"There's enough there to pay for my drinks, one for you, and one for anyone else in your place. I won't start any trouble. But I don't back down from anyone." His cool, green eyes held those of the sutler.

The sutler reddened and then his mouth tightened. He reached beneath the bar and came up with a double-barreled shotgun and, cocking it as it levered across the bar, he pointed it at the table where the other three men sat.

"Fellers, if you don't get Rufe out of here in one minute, I'm turnin' this old scattergun loose on that table. I purely hate that table an' if someone is still settin' there when I shoot, I won't be responsible fer their hides." The black bore of the shotgun drew down upon the table and the three men scattered.

"Rufe," one of them yelled, "back off! That feller ain't causin' you no trouble an' this is the only bar we kin belly up to fer fifty miles. 'Sides, that

shotgun looks purely sinful from where I stand."

"Move on outside," said the sutler grimly. "When you can act right, you're welcome to come back in." The sutler did not lower the gun. One of the men seized Rufe by the arm and another pushed him from the back, forcing him through the door.

The sutler looked at Bonner and at the coin he had placed on the bar. "Thanks, stranger, but I don't drink my own stuff. Ain't good fer business. But, I'll pour you another."

Bonner shook his head. "Two's enough. I have a feelin' that when I walk through that door there'll be a reception waitin' for me."

"Reckon so," said the sutler. "Don't sell short that big-mouthed one they call Rufe. An' keep yore eyes peeled fer th' other'ns, too."

Bonner nodded and turning, walked to the door. He paused and the sutler watched as he bent and carefully tied the leather thongs dangling from the

end of the holster. He's a shootist, all right, thought the sutler. There's gonna be lead flyin' soon as he steps through the door.

★ ★ ★

"Rufe." One of the man's friends stepped to front the gunman and forced his gaze to turn to him. Rufe was staring at the sutler's door, his hand hovering over his gunbutt.

"Rufe, I think we'd better let this one go. I heerd about someone who was relation to old John Wesley Hardin, an' it was said he was even better than the old man. Why don't we just walk away frum this one ant ferget about it?"

The gunman shook his head. "Nope. We're gonna get him. You two spread out on either side of the porch. I'll face 'im when he comes out. One of us is shore to get 'im."

The man shrugged and looked at his companion. The other turned and walked to one side of the porch, not

noticeably enthusiastically in favor of the plan.

With his two companions placed to his advantage, Rufe straightened and faced the doorway. This man Bonner was his meat. Other shootists would now think twice before bracing Rufe.

★ ★ ★

The woman excused herself to begin preparing a meal for Captain Bellows and the guests. Clara stepped out upon the porch of the small house. It was oppressively hot, the late afternoon sun beating down upon the post, of necessity, for security, made barren of trees, leaving no shade.

She wondered where Bonner had been taken for the evening and night. He would spend the time, she thought, smoking and talking with the men present. Perhaps take a drink at the sutler's store. The thought caused her to look in the direction of the store.

One man faced the open doorway

of the building; another stood at the end of the narrow porch, also watching the door. It was then she noticed another man crouched, half-hidden at the corner of the building opposite the one at the end of the porch. She had been around the camp of the Indians ten years or more of her life and recognized a trap being set. For whom?

For Bonner? A chill ran up her back. Coolly she stepped back into the room she had just left. The woman came to the kitchen door and looked questioningly at her.

Clara did not answer her look, but went to her cot and took her rifle from beneath it. Jacking a shell into the chamber she spoke to the woman.

"There is trouble on the street in front of the sutler's store. You had better stay inside."

Without looking at the woman again, Clara stepped out upon the porch. Quickly she sized up the tableau before her. One man poised before the door,

an expectant leer on his face; one at the end of the porch, holding a six-gun cocked, poised and ready. The final man crouched at the corner of the building, a rifle in his hands, watching for Rufe's signal.

Bonner's shadow moved back of the doorway and then he stepped out, entirely exposed, facing Rufe.

"Todd, the corner!" Clara screamed. Rufe, startled, thrust down and came up with his six-gun firing. The man with the cocked six-gun brought it up and as he did so, Bonner's hands flashed and came up, his gun bellowing.

Rufe's first shot hit the doorframe beside Bonner. Before he could fire the second time Bonner's bullet slammed into his chest, and the second one caught the man with the rifle as he slipped beyond the shelter of the porch to fire. A neat blue hole appeared above his eyes and he rolled over from his crouch, the rifle dropping from his hands.

Clara drew down upon the one with the six-gun levering at Bonner, and as Bonner's shot sent Rufe to his knees, she fired. The man whirled with the impact, stared at the blood spurting from his chest and staggered over to lean against the side of the building. He dropped his gun and, raising his head, glared at Rufe, his hands pressed to his bleeding chest.

"You . . . you got us all kilt, Rufe . . . all . . . kilt . . . " His eyes glazed and he slid sideways, quivering in his last moments of life.

Dying from Bonner's slug in the chest, yet Rufe heard the voice of his companion. With fog gathering about him, his eyes already dimming, he struggled to his knees. With his left hand he raised himself, then fell to his elbows, his head sagging, the shaggy hair grey with the dirt of the street.

Blood dripped from his mouth as he slowly drew his gun from leather, having never gotten the weapon from his holster. His entire body shaking,

he seized the six-gun with both hands. The barrel wavered and dipped as he attempted to line it on the figure now standing on the edge of the sutler's porch.

"Todd, he's going to shoot again!" Clara's voice broke the sudden stillness surrounding the death drama being enacted under burning sun and in inch-deep dust of the ground.

At the sound of the shots the corporal of the guard was called out. Captain Bellows rushed out upon the porch of his office just as Clara fired at the man with the six-gun drawing down upon Bonner. The officer stood stock still, his mouth sagging, eyes bulging at the tableau before him.

Rufe's eyes squinted along the barrel of his gun. Bonner was a wavering figure in deepening haze. He gritted his teeth and growling low in his throat, shakily eared back the hammer to the weapon.

"Bonner!" Clara screamed at him. She cocked the rifle and levered it at

Rufe, but Bonner stepped from the porch and shook his head at her.

"No," he said softly, his words carrying across the open space like a whisper of wind in a pine. "Don't shoot," he said.

Slowly, almost thoughtfully, he stepped from the porch and walked toward Rufe. His hands hung by his sides, his six-gun reloaded and back in leather. His eyes never left the face of the dying gunman. He stopped a few feet in front of Rufe and stood looking down at him.

"You killed us all," Rufe gulped, through a mouthful of blood and saliva. "Three of us an' we didn't even touch you." The dust-covered head rolled back so the bleared eyes could look upward into Bonner's face. "Bein' that fast, you must be ol' Wesley's kin, huh?"

Bonner did not answer.

"Damn you, talk to me! You've killed me, now tell me who you are!"

"I'm a rancher from Sundance,

Dakota Territory," Bonner said quietly. He stooped and pushed the gun barrel aside. "Who I am other than that is not important. What is important is that you are dyin'. Is there anyone you want notified? Family? Kin?"

The gun slipped from Rufe's fingers, and Bonner took it and lowered the hammer, then pushed the gun into Rufe's holster. The man's eyes glared then glazed. He grunted and fell forward, face down in the dust. Rufe had gone to meet his two companions, wherever that might be.

Sighing, Bonner looked down at the man a long moment and then turning, walked to the post commander. He took his six-gun and handed it out to Captain Bellows, butt first.

"I apologize, Captain, for what had happened here. I did not start it, but I don't back away from trouble when it faces me." The sutler had hurried across the street as Bonner was speaking.

The captain waved his hand. "Put

away your iron, Bonner." He turned to the sutler. "What happened, Morgan?"

The sutler nodded toward the three corpses. "They started harrawin' Bonner here. They was insultin' about the lady, too." He glanced at Clara. "Bonner just done what any red-blooded man would do, defend the honor of a good woman an' hisself."

"I suspected as much," he said. He turned to the sergeant-major of the post who had arrived and stood back of the captain. "Sergeant-Major, see that the bodies are taken to the aid-station and have the doc prepare them for burial. We'll put them in Boot Hill tomorrow morning, early." The captain spoke to Clara and Bonner. "I suspect supper is about ready. Go on over to my quarters and I'll join you as soon as I get the post to bed."

16

THE afternoon drifted from oppressive heat into a cool evening. The fort was quiet. Sentries stood at or paced their posts. There was a muted murmur of slowed down activity. The sun touched the edges of the parade ground and dropped, leaving pink brushing the skies, and a few tufted clouds slowly turned rose and then into gentle fading colors as dusk invaded.

Supper finished, Clara helped the women do the dishes and rearrange the kitchen. The two men sat on the small porch overlooking the parade ground and smoked and talked.

Leaving Bellows' living-quarters, Bonner and Clara walked together around the parade ground. The boardwalk skirted the officers' quarters and squared at the corners of the parade

ground. As they walked their shoulders brushed together from time to time.

Bonner was vitally aware of the woman beside him. Young and vibrant, not beautiful, but pleasantly featured. She had suffered ten years of captivity and some harshness with the tribe that held her. But mainly she had come through the ordeal without impairment of mind or body. He was deeply drawn to her and would never forget their days on the dark trail together. That she was leaving in a few days brought a strange, seldom experienced ache to his heart.

They paused momentarily before turning to retrace their steps in the gently enclosing darkness of the compound. Lights were coming on in the quarters. Shadowy figures passed before and through the mellow streams coming from the windows.

He faced her and reaching out took her hand. It rested in his palm trustingly. She looked up at him, her eyes dark in the gathering dusk.

"You leave for Indiana, for home,

shortly," he said slowly. He hesitated. "I will miss you, Clara."

Her face lowered momentarily and she stared at the ground. Then she raised her head and the yellow glow from a window nearby glistened upon tears on her cheeks.

"I will miss you, too, Todd," she murmured. Then she moved closer to him and rested her head against his chest. He put his arms about her and for long moments they remained that way. She heard the heavy, slow rhythm of his strong heart, felt the intake and exhale from the deep chest. His arms about her felt protective and the scent of manhood, his tobacco, the shirt, a slight aroma of sweat, all mingled, filled her senses. Here was a man she might . . .

She raised her head and moved away gently. "I must go in now," she whispered. Taking his face between her palms, she raised on tiptoe and kissed him, a slow, sweet pressure upon his lips, a quick, tingly touch of tongue

to tongue, a momentary caress. Then she turned and still holding his hand, walked with him to the quarters where she was to spend the next few days.

Bonner woke several times during the night. He called to mind the sweetness of her kiss, the soft, full pressure of her breasts against him, the momentary touch of her fingers upon his cheeks. She was fully woman, ripe with life, ready to give to her man the completeness of her womanhood . . . she could be a lifetime companion, a woman to love completely, be a mother to his two growing children . . . and bring him sons and daughters of their own . . .

★ ★ ★

It was midnight. Bonner was drowsing, having dreamed and awakened. He slept in a bunk near the door of the quarters assigned him. His name was called softly. He sat up. Dreaming or real? It came again, a whisper.

"Bonner . . . Bonner . . . "

Rising, he drew on his pants and stepped to the door. Clara stood in the shadows, her eyes luminous in the faint light of the stars.

"What is it, Clara?" He stepped closer to her and took her hand.

During the night she felt the fullness of her reluctance to return to a dimly remembered farm in Indiana. The strong man she had lived with along the dark trail from Laramie drew her. The thought of living on a ranch, safe and secure for the first time she could recall, was a good feeling.

With Bonner? Suddenly she knew her desire lay there. She took his hand in both of hers and drew him to her, looking up into his eyes. She took in the seriousness of his face, the strong planes of his features as he looked down at her with concern.

She lay her head against his chest and her arms about his neck. His arms tightened about her.

"I want to stay with you, Todd," she

murmured. "Take me to your ranch, as housekeeper, as companion to your children, or as your wife. In whatever way you will have me there. I want only to be with you for the rest of my life."

He drew her closer. "I am slow with words, Clara," he said. "I was tryin' to find them to say what would persuade you to stay. I find I have a real love for you an' I want you as my wife."

His lips lowered to hers and he kissed her, long and passionately, and felt her response in the strength of her arms and the sweetness of her lips.

* * *

They were married in the chapel at Fort Sully. Captain Bellows stood beside Bonner and the housekeeper stood up with Clara. When the ceremony was over Captain Bellows wrapped Clara in his arms and kissed her cheek.

"If this cowpoke don't treat you right, Mrs Bonner," he said whimsically,

"you let me know and I'll straighten him out."

"Be happy, my dear," murmured the woman who hugged her closely. "Be happy; love and be loved, but above all, be happy!"

Having run low on supplies along the dark trail, they were outfitted again for the trip south through the badlands and on to Bonner's ranch near the small town of Sundance. Knowing the country fairly well from this point, Bonner brought them through with little trouble. They traveled slow. Summer was upon the land and while some days were hot, others were pleasant and nights were bright with moon and stars.

In the time from Fort Sully to Sundance they learned about each other. She learned fully of Bonner's former wife, Nina, and the two children awaiting them. Adam who was soon to be six years old, and Amanda, who had just turned three. The thought had come to her, she was a mother,

and had, a few nights ago, experienced the wonder and beauty of knowing the rushing heart and tingling sweetness for the first time made fully woman.

She had met Bonner in their blankets in Bellows' quarters and even now was awed at the sweetness and wonder of the meeting of two bodies in such gentleness and love, in the depth of moving together and feeling the trembling urge to receive him fully as a woman. She blushed at the thought of it and looked over at her man and found his eyes on her, solemn and speaking with lights that told her he was thinking her thoughts.

As he had come to her the first night, she had held him away, her hands upon his chest. "I must tell you, Todd, before we go any further — "

"You don't have to tell me anything, Clara. What is past is past — "

"That I have never known a man. My Indian father would not allow the young men to touch me. Why, I do not know, for other white women became

playthings for any man who wanted them. I think, perhaps, it was because of his wife, Red Leaf. She was never affectionate, but she was never cruel. Later, the old man needed me to keep his meals coming and his lodge clean, helping with his young daughter."

"I never questioned that part of your life, Clara," he said gently. "You could not help what did or did not happen to you as a captive. You are very fortunate that the family of One-Who-Leaps-Highest took you as a slave."

It was the last said concerning that part of her life. They loved fully and completely and he, an experienced male, once married and having known other women now and then, knew after their first night together that she had come to him as a virgin.

17

HE lay beneath a narrow overhanging ledge in the heights of the Sundance Hills. His black, glinting eyes searched the flats before him and the buildings of the ranch spread out beyond the flats. It was a large ranch, with corrals, barns, sheds, and a large, rambling house, shaded on all sides by live-oak and pine. There was movement there as men worked the corrals of horses, moved about the barns and sheds, and came in from the range and rode out from time to time.

Beyond the hills and behind him was a small town. Sundance he knew it was called. That meant little to him, for he was Cheyenne and knew very little of the white man's language. But he knew enough to follow the man he sought, and had come to kill.

The man had taken his woman, had shamed him before his tribe. Now he sought revenge and had searched the Black Hills and beyond until he found his enemy's trail.

Cold Star lay and watched and waited.

★ ★ ★

Adam took Clara's entry into the family matter-of-factly. He looked up at Clara after being introduced as Todd's new wife. After a long minute, he nodded.

"Are you going to be our ma?" he asked.

Clara knelt and gravely met his look. "I am going to be your best friend and try to do the things a mother might do for you," she said.

"Like cookin' our meals?" he asked. He glanced at his father. "Pa is a turrible cook."

Clara laughed. "He may be a better cook than I. But, I will do my best and you and Amanda can help me."

Amanda was shy. She hid behind the skirts of the woman who had looked after them while Bonner was away. It was several days before she came willingly into Clara's arms. But once there, she squeezed Clara's neck tightly and there came words that remained in Clara's heart for the rest of her days.

"I'm glad you came home, Mommy," she whispered. "I missed you so."

Clara's eyes misted and she hugged the little girl tightly and lovingly. "I have missed you, too, Amanda," she said, "so very much."

★ ★ ★

Clara settled into life on the Bar-B ranch. Once she learned the routine she was busy every day. She found time to play with Amanda and to listen to Adam practise reading from a tattered primer. He would begin school in the autumn in Sundance. The little town was five miles away, along Sundance creek.

The woman who had cared for the house and for the children during Todd's absence was, in fact, the wife of one of the cowhands on the ranch. She worked regularly as maid and housekeeper in the big house. There was also a Mexican woman, wife of the ranch's wrangler, who did the heavier cleaning and washing. She also helped in the kitchen when the evening meal was being prepared

Clara was suddenly part of the ongoing routine of every day. She fell in love with the children and realized one evening, as she sat watching Todd solemnly teaching Adam how to braid a lariat, that she was deeply and completely in love with the man. She was committed to him and realized she would have it no other way and, while he had never put it into direct words, she was certain he felt the same about her.

The ranch became her life and weeks passed quickly. She as quickly learned the routine of the white woman in

civilization. She shopped for essentials with the housekeeper guiding her selections. She learned the prices of articles and that a list was kept of her purchases, which Todd paid for monthly, or when he went into town.

It was only a few days following her arrival that Bonner came to the house in the middle of a warm afternoon. Riding beside him, astride her horse as Indian women rode, and which Clara had learned was not unusual for white women, was a pretty woman in men's pants and a plaid shirt. A low-crowned, broad-brimmed hat covered her dark hair.

Clara met them at the door. Bonner ushered the woman into the room. The visitor removed her hat and smiled gravely at Clara.

"This is our closest neighbor, Clara," said Bonner. "This is Rachel Manning. It was her husband who was killed and I tracked the killer to Red Bluff, Wyoming. I wanted you to meet her."

Rachel Manning smiled, her face

lighting up with an inner glow. "It is my pleasure to meet you, Clara. When Todd came back with a wife, the entire community was abuzz. Now that I have met you I can see why he wouldn't come home without you."

Clara blushed. "Thank you for coming to visit," she murmured. "There is so much yet for me to learn about caring for a white man's lodge — house." Todd grinned as she used the Cheyenne word for house or home.

"I can see he made a good choice. And now Adam and Amanda have someone to mother them."

Suddenly Clara realized here was a woman seeking her friendship. She took her hand and led her to a settee on one side of the room.

"I'll get us some coffee and donuts and you tell me what I need to know about caring for this man who found me in the wilderness," she said.

Bonner grinned at them. "I see you have a lot to talk about, so I'll be out at the corrals. Tell me when you're ready

to go, Rachel, and I'll send one of the men with you."

Rachel Manning nodded gravely. "I think I can find my way, but I'll let you know," she said. Bonner left the room, feeling good about having brought the woman to meet Clara so soon after her arrival. Rachel Manning could do much in helping his Indian-reared wife to settle into the white-man's world.

★ ★ ★

Bill Shadley was foreman of the Bar-B Ranch. He had been on the spread when it belonged to Bonner and his first wife. At the moment he was troubled about some strange occurrences he had detected about the ranch.

He came to where Bonner leaned on the top pole of a corral watching Raoul Manchez, the ranch wrangler, work with a yearling mare. Bonner wanted the mare gentled for Clara to use.

"Todd, you gotta minute?"

"Always for you, Bill. What's on your mind?"

The two men eased away from the corral and squatted in the shade of a nearby tack shed. Bonner took out a bag of Bull Durham and handed it to the foreman. Quietly, at ease with each other after long years of close contact on a job they both knew so well, they rolled cigarettes and lit them.

Drawing in a deep breath, Shadley let smoke trickle from his lips and nose before answering.

"There's somethin' strange goin' on, Todd. Somethin' odd. I can't rightly put a finger on it."

"What makes you think that?" asked Todd, eyeing his foreman. He trusted Bill Shadley implicitly and knew the man would not come to him unless concerned.

"Josh Creely, one of the young hoss handlers, said he seen moccasin tracks around one of th' hoss corrals an' also around one of the tack sheds."

"Indian tracks, he thinks?" asked

Todd, drawing on his smoke and letting it out slowly.

"Well, this kid never ever saw Indian tracks, I guess. He thought it might be someone wearing soft-soled shoes."

Bonner turned it over in his mind. He knew Clara still had her Indian garb, moccasins, deerskin skirt and waist, and headband. But she would never go out at night about the corrals. Besides, she was always with him at night, cuddled against him, sleeping soundly, or turning to him in love.

He shook his head. "There hasn't been Indians around this area for a long time," he said. "That doesn't mean there couldn't be. Maybe some renegade from the fighting up north, working his way back to the reservation, or just passing through to someplace else."

"Maybe thinkin' about stealin' him a hoss to make his trip faster," Shadley mused.

"Maybe," said Bonner. "Have some of the boys get up a watch about the

corrals for several nights. Two hours each. That won't disturb their next day's work too much."

"Not near as much as ridin' into town to visit some little gal," Shadley said, grinning. "We'll do that tonight." He paused and then continued, "One other thing, Todd. One of the boys ridin' the foothills back there come up on a cow mooin' around a wadi. He worked his way down and found a six-month-old calf, ours, killed and butchered and then slung into the ditch. Th' old maw cow wouldn't leave until he roped an' dragged her halfway back to th' herd."

Bonner turned this over in his mind. Indian tracks around the corrals. A butchered calf. He raised his eyes and looked at the blue line of hills above the ranch that lay in a large, gently sloped basin. Who or what was there watching the ranch? A cold chill eased up his spine.

★ ★ ★

Over a small fire, with the smoke filtering up to disappear among the pines surrounding the shallow cave he camped in, Cold Star prepared the meat of the young calf. Thin strips smoked for several days and dried in the hot sun became jerky which lasted for a long time.

There were roots and berries in the hills and fish in Sundance Creek. He was eating well and waiting and watching the ranch. Several times he had seen Clara about the big house, on the porch, walking with Bonner to the corrals, or with one of the women working in a large garden back of the house.

Hatred was a worm eating at his heart when he saw the man and woman together. He had lusted after her for a lifetime. And now, she had given herself to the man he hated most in the world.

Time would come, he knew, when he and the white man would fight to the death. He had already scouted the

corrals of the ranch and knew it would be no task to steal a horse. He would steal two horses, he mused, and take the woman with him. After he had fully satisfied himself with her he would give her to his friends to do with as they wished.

He watched and waited and fumed, counting the time when he would be able to go down into the ranch openly, face the woman and the man, and satisfy the canker that ate at his soul more with each rising sun.

★ ★ ★

Clara was not a superstitious person. She had seen Cold Star fall, had seen him lying in the blood of his wound around his head. Cold Star was gone and would never again disrupt her life with his sneers, his touches, his threatening of what he would do if she did not yield herself to him. All this she knew.

Yet when she looked across the flats

227

of the ranch, down the valleys, seeing the tranquillity of the land, the green graze meadows dotted with selected breeds of cattle, she felt an unease. What if . . .

She shook her head and scolded herself for such thoughts. There was no way he could be alive. She must put those thoughts from her. But deep in the night, with her man breathing deeply in rest beside her, she thought of those days and prayed what she had seen in the village of Buffalo Man was correct: Cold Star was dead.

Knowing that Bonner thought the Indian dead and out of their lives, she did not bring the subject up. One time, confiding her fears and relating of her life with the Cheyenne to Rachel Manning, now a close friend, she mentioned Cold Star and her continued thinking and fear of him.

"Put him out of your mind," her new friend told her. "From what you tell me, the man was killed. You are safe here, with a man you love,

with children to rear, and a life that will bring you love, happiness and satisfaction. Dwell on that and put these other shadows where they belong, in the memories of days now past."

She knew her friend was right. The blue hills she looked at so often, and the smiling fields of the ranch, the voices of the children, all formed something that should help her put away forever those ghosts of yesterday.

But now and then, at moments least expected, the snarling face of Cold Star entered her mind and cold shivers shook her, bringing haunting fear and doubt.

18

FOUR ranches ran cattle on ranges bordering each other in the Sundance Basin where the Bar-B spread lay. Two of the ranchers were near the size of the Bar-B, with cattle to the south and west of Bonner's spread. One ranch, the W and R, belonging to Rachel Manning, much smaller, lay to the north.

Round-up was in mid-October and April. Herds were gathered and strays belonging to other brands were hazed on to their home ranges. The ranchers co-operated in this, as was done throughout the cattle country. It was a time-honored tradition and each helped the other in running the round-up as smoothly and efficiently as possible.

"I'll be spending most of my time on the range until the round-up is over," Todd explained to Clara. This

was her first experience of such, and she questioned the purpose and reason for his protracted absence.

"Cattle have a way of straying from their range and this is our way of seeing that each rancher gets a correct count of his herds. Also new calves are branded, along with mavericks."

She was uneasy when the men all rode out at first light the morning of the beginning of the round-up. Four men were left at the ranch to care for the chores, and to keep the horse herd fresh and ready for remounts when needed. An elderly cook for the crew was taken out to the round-up with the chuck-wagon, leaving the Mexican woman and the housekeeper to cook for the men left behind.

Even with the four men and two women around her, Clara was still uneasy. There was a dread in her heart when Todd was not near. It was an unknown dread that from time to time sent her to the front porch and lifted her eyes to the blue line

of the Sundance Hills. She paced the porch and the living-room of the big house each day, wishing the round-up finished and Todd once again by her side.

From his high vantage point in the hills Cold Star saw the departure of the men from the ranch. He waited and saw no one return. The second day two men came in and replaced tired horses with fresh mounts from the corral and left. He counted the four men about the buildings and the two women who were usually about the house with Clara. His eyes gleamed. The time was here!

★ ★ ★

Bonner also was uneasy. He glanced often at the hills and recalled the report of the moccasin tracks about the corrals. The butchered calf had not been explained. The fourth day of the round-up he left Bill Shadley in charge and mounting his horse, headed for the

ranch house. The dread of something happening ate deep in his mind. He wished to race the horse, but knew the miles would pass beneath them at a steady lope, without exhausting the animal halfway there, and his having to walk the rest of the way.

* * *

After her midday meal Clara lay down with a book. Rachel Manning and her son Bruce had come by and taken the children with them into Sundance. It would be late before they returned. In a few minutes the book was laid aside and she dozed in the heat of the autumn day. She woke suddenly.

Usually Rosa, the Mexican woman, hummed at her work about the house. There was no voice humming. The housekeeper was not a quiet woman and her footsteps clattered as she scurried through the house. The house was still. Usually she heard the men working about the barns and sheds,

around the corrals, talking amongst themselves and to the horses. She did not hear them. A stillness lay upon the house and barns. She rose and sat on the edge of the bed.

"Girl-With-Feet-Of-Deer woman now." As the grating words reached her she screamed and leaped from the bed.

He stood in the doorway. His chest was bare except for a cord about his neck upon which was strung claws of a bear, killed in his youth and part of his totem. He wore the Cheyenne pants and leggings, with a breech-clout before his thighs. About him was a leather belt into which was thrust a white man's steel hatchet, and opposite it a deerskin sheath from which the handle of a long knife protruded. He was tall and powerful and his eyes, fastened upon Clara, were glinting with hatred and satisfaction. Cold Star had found the woman he had sought for weeks and months.

"I . . . I am not alone here, Cold

Star," she said in his tongue, the language of her childhood. "If they find you they will kill you."

A grimace of a smile twisted his lips and he shook his head. "You and I are the only ones alive in these barns and house," he said. "You are mine now to do as I wish."

Despair rose in her mind. Rosa and the housekeeper, dead? "There are four cowboys — "

He continued to shake his head. "White men are so careless. It was child's play to kill them. And the white woman and the Mexican — weak, weak. Not strong and fighting like Cheyenne women."

"You've killed them all," she said softly. She dropped her head and tears coursed down her cheeks. "I am the cause of their deaths." She raised her head and looked at him.

"Why, Cold Star? Why? I am not worth such sacrifice on their part. And you cannot want me as your woman now. I have been this man's woman

for several months."

He nodded. "You are right. I want only to show the white men that this man cannot be treated as dirt, and that I can destroy them and theirs when and where I wish."

"Revenge?" she whispered, brokenly, her hands twisting in her apron.

"Yes, revenge," he said gratingly. "You and the white men left me bleeding and unconscious. You thought this man was dead. But I lived and escaped on the trail to the reservation. I joined the wild ones who refused to go with the white soldiers. And I trailed you and your white man here for revenge!"

She was deeply frightened. But her mind was casting about thinking of a way to escape this evil that stood in her house. She was an excellent shot with rifle and not bad with the six-gun. But there were no guns in the bedroom.

She felt his eyes upon her, searching her form, as though she were undressed. Apparently he had been without a

woman for a long time and he was remembering the lust he had felt for her as a young man lusts for a young woman.

The thought sickened her but she raised her head and looked at him, calmed now by a thought. "Cold Star, I have never loved you. You know that my father would not give me to you. But now I am a woman, no longer a foolish girl. If you wish me, I will go with you as your concubine, your slave. I will sleep in your blankets, cook your meals, carry your water, care for your horses, if you will leave here and not harm the white man I have married."

He grimaced. "Why should I promise anything? Besides, I will fight this man and kill him, then I will do with you as I wish." But his lust had risen and he left the doorway and approached her.

"Remove those white woman's clothes and I will show you how an Indian brave treats a squaw who scorns him." He stripped the belt from his waist and tossed it into the rocking chair, striding

across the room toward her.

Clara twisted and leaping on the bed threw herself against the wall away from him. She seized a small vase from a stand.

"I will not be raped," she told him in Cheyenne. "I will fight you to the end. I told you my proposition and that is the only way you can have me!"

He growled in his throat and sprang across the bed at her. As she dodged he caught her apron and ripped it from her. She twisted and struck at him with the vase, but he grunted and slapped it aside.

He seized her and threw her on to the bed and with brute force yanked her dress above her waist. She fought him, slapping and clawing at his bare chest, her fingernails bringing bloody stripes. But he laughed at her and slowly subdued her and with his iron knees forced her legs apart.

Kneeling over her he laughed. It was the first time she could recall ever hearing laughter from the cruel slit

of his mouth. However, it was not laughter of mirth, but of derision and triumph.

"Ha! Girl-With-Feet-Of-Deer cannot run now, can she! You outran me as a youth, you escaped me as a young woman. But now I am going to have you as I desire and you will die having known what an Indian brave is capable of doing in his blankets!"

She screamed then, long and hard and wailing. She thrashed beneath him, striking and kicking, clawing and spitting. But he was too strong, too in control. Grinning evilly, he reached for the cord that held up his pants. Grinning at her, his eyes gleaming in lust, he slowly began releasing the knot of the cord.

★ ★ ★

"*Clara!*"

As he swept into the yard before the house, Bonner shouted her name. He leaped from the saddle as the exhausted

horse was still moving. He shouted her name again and bounded up on to the porch.

His quick glance saw the tumbled body of the housekeeper just inside the open door that led into the front room. A quick turn of his head saw the sprawled, bloody body of one of the men by the gate of the nearest corral. The quietness of the place told him of tragedy and danger. Heedless of either he leaped to the doorway.

The bare-chested Cold Star met him at the door, blood dripping from Clara's clawing. In his right hand was the hatchet and in the other the long skinning knife. He glared at Bonner.

"They are all dead, white man," he said gutturally in Cheyenne, which Bonner did not understand. Words, however, were not necessary to convey the man's intent. Seeing the sprawled, lifeless body of the housekeeper, and the one man near the corral, Bonner, in deepest despair, assumed everyone was dead, including Clara.

Slowly he backed from the porch. His six-gun, wrapped in the belt, was in his saddle-bag. He did not wear it during the heavy, busy work of the round-up. His rifle was in the saddle sheath. If he could reach it before the Indian attacked . . .

He stepped off the porch, his eyes narrowed, his body tensed for the attack he knew was coming.

"I thought you were dead," he said softly, knowing the Indian did not speak his language. But Cold Star instinctively understood the tone and the words.

"I am here," he thumbed his chest with the knife hand. "I have come to kill you and the woman." He stepped from the doorway and eased to the edge of the porch.

"This man will leave you in your blood as you left me, but I was alive and you will be dead!"

With words he screamed his hatred and launched himself at Bonner!

19

HEARING Bonner shout her name, Cold Star paused in his preparation to ravage Clara. He glared at her and then viciously slapping her, knocking her half-unconscious, he quickly adjusted his clothes and seizing his hatchet and knife from the chair, raced to the front door.

Clara lay dazed. She had heard Bonner shout her name and knew a surge of joy that he had arrived. Now she was trying to gain full consciousness. Bonner would not be expecting the Indian and would be killed. She struggled with her swimming mind and dazedness, and slowly regained sight and consciousness.

She knew Cold Star had not had his way with her; for this she was relieved. But that he was about to harm the one to whom she had given her life and

heart was enough to bring her sharply alert. What could she do?

She rose and swayed and quickly recalled the rifle in the front room over the mantle. Always loaded, the rifle was kept ready for an emergency. She struggled with her balance, and with what seemed excruciating slowness, made her way into the hall and into the front room. She stood, swaying with weakness, looking for the Indian.

Cold Star stood in the doorway, his back to her, but as she entered the room, he slipped to the edge of the porch and with a scream, launched himself bodily at Bonner.

Seizing the rifle, she staggered to the doorway and leaned against the frame, breathing heavily. Her heart lurched as she saw Bonner beneath the half-naked body of the Indian. He held Cold Star's wrist, keeping the gleaming blade of the hatchet from chopping into his body.

The Indian was powerful. He jerked back and loosened Bonner's grip on his wrist. He swung the hatchet back

and, with a yell, chopped downward at Bonner's head.

With supreme effort, the white man bucked and kicked, throwing the Indian off his stroke. The hatchet buried itself into the hardpan beside Bonner's head. Bonner twisted and threw a straight right fist upward that connected with the Indian's chin. Cold Star grunted and slumped back and Bonner slipped from beneath him and staggered to his feet.

Dazed and winded from the effort of wrestling with the Indian, Bonner staggered towards the porch. Leaping to his feet, Cold Star screamed in anger and sprang toward Bonner, brandishing his knife and holding it for a gutting, upward stroke, the true stance of one experienced in knife fighting.

"Todd!" Clara screamed and tossed the rifle toward him, the sun glinting dully off the blue-steel barrel. Todd grunted as he half caught the weapon, the heavy stock thudding into his chest. The Indian was upon him. White

teeth bared in a grimace, eyes glinting with hate and triumph, Cold Star swept the knife upward, pointing toward Bonner's groin. Bonner stepped back, tripping backwards as his knees struck the porch. The rifle slipped between his legs and caught the impact of the knife.

Bonner rolled, coming to his knees, levering a shell into the rifle. Cold Star was upon him, driving the knife toward his chest! Bonner thrust the rifle into the Indian's naked lower belly, and pulled the trigger, sending a blast of lead through his groin.

The knife entered Bonner's shoulder deeply and he fell to the floor. Grunting with pain and struggling, he levered another shell into the rifle and pulled the trigger. The bore was buried against Cold Star's chest and as it exploded, the Indian screamed and rolled aside, shot through the lungs and heart, a gaping hole in his back as the round ripped through his body.

The Indian struggled to his knees,

blood pouring from his chest and groin. He groaned and looked upward at Clara who stood, her hands over her mouth, her eyes wide and staring, watching the nemesis of her girlhood and youth die before her.

Cold Star rolled to his back and his eyes glared at her in the last moment of his life. They dulled and became sightless and his chest heaved with one last breath. He was dead.

Bonner lay on his back with blood escaping around the knife. Shaking, dazed from the scenes of pain and horror, Clara knelt beside him. Grimacing and gritting her teeth, she seized the haft of the knife and pulling with all her strength removed it from Bonner's shoulder.

He groaned with the pain and sweat broke out on his face. Blood poured from the wound, blackening his shirt. With the knife she quickly cut his shirt from his chest and shoulder, baring the wound.

Making a flat bandage from part of

the shirt, she pressed it on to the wound and, ripping a strip from the cloth, bound it in place.

"Now," she said, shakily, "let's get you inside and on the bed, so I can take care of that cut properly. The wound is deep."

"Is the Indian dead?" Bonner asked, in an equally shaky voice.

"Yes. It is Cold Star. How he found us we'll never know. But he won't bother either of us again."

He sighed and shook his head. "Clara Bonner," he said weakly, with a slight grimace the might be judged an attempt to smile, "you are such a woman!"

* * *

The round-up was over. Bonner was able to ride the last few days and on the final day Clara left the children with Rachel Manning at her small ranch, and accompanied Bonner to the grounds where the branding was coming to an end.

They sat on their mounts on a small rise overlooking the round-up. Chuck wagons were being loaded. Wranglers were working the remudas separating the horse herds, and pointing them out toward their various ranges; branding fires were being extinguished and personal mounts loaded with gear for the trip into the respective ranches.

Clara sighed and reaching over linked her arm with Bonner's. "This will be our life, won't it, Todd? Cattle and horses, working and sharing the work."

He pressed her arm to him and looking down into her face saw the love and trust mirrored there. "This, and some trips to some cities to buy you new dresses, now and then."

"And baby clothes?" she murmured.

He stared at her. "Baby — ? Are you trying to tell me something?"

There was a smug look on her face when she answered. "What are you going to name your son when he comes in April or May?"

With a shout he pulled her from the saddle into his arms and those around the nearest wagons wondered about their boss, kissing his wife right out in the open before God and everybody!

But others saw, shrugged and grinned and allowed he was boss and if he wanted the world to see him kiss his wife in the open he could.

And Clara agreed!

THE END

Other titles in the Linford Western Library:

TOP HAND
Wade Everett

The Broken T was big. But no ranch is big enough to let a man hide from himself.

GUN WOLVES OF LOBO BASIN
Lee Floren

The Feud was a blood debt. When Smoke Talbot found the outlaws who gunned down his folks he aimed to nail their hide to the barn door.

SHOTGUN SHARKEY
Marshall Grover

The westbound coach carrying the indomitable Larry and Stretch headed for a shooting showdown.

FIGHTING RAMROD
Charles N. Heckelmann

Most men would have cut their losses, but Frazer counted the bullets in his guns and said he'd soak the range in blood before he'd give up another inch of what was his.

LONE GUN
Eric Allen

Smoke Blackbird had been away too long. The Lequires had seized the Blackbird farm, forcing the Indians and settlers off, and no one seemed willing to fight! He had to fight alone.

THE THIRD RIDER
Barry Cord

Mel Rawlins wasn't going to let anything stand in his way. His father was murdered, his two brothers gone. Now Mel rode for vengeance.

ARIZONA DRIFTERS
W. C. Tuttle

When drifting Dutton and Lonnie Steelman decide to become partners they find that they have a common enemy in the formidable Thurston brothers.

TOMBSTONE
Matt Braun

Wells Fargo paid Luke Starbuck to outgun the silver-thieving stagecoach gang at Tombstone. Before long Luke can see the only thing bearing fruit in this eldorado will be the gallows tree.

HIGH BORDER RIDERS
Lee Floren

Buckshot McKee and Tortilla Joe cut the trail of a border tough who was running Mexican beef into Texas. They stopped the smuggler in his tracks.

BRETT RANDALL, GAMBLER
E. B. Mann

Larry Day had the choice of running away from the law or of assuming a dead man's place. No matter what he decided he was bound to end up dead.

THE GUNSHARP
William R. Cox

The Eggerleys weren't very smart. They trained their sights on Will Carney and Arizona's biggest blood bath began.

THE DEPUTY OF SAN RIANO
Lawrence A. Keating and
Al. P. Nelson

When a man fell dead from his horse, Ed Grant was spotted riding away from the scene. The deputy sheriff rode out after him and came up against everything from gunfire to dynamite.

FARGO: MASSACRE RIVER
John Benteen

The ambushers up ahead had now blocked the road. Fargo's convoy was a jumble, a perfect target for the insurgents' weapons!

SUNDANCE: DEATH IN THE LAVA
John Benteen

The Modoc's captured the wagon train and its cargo of gold. But now the halfbreed they called Sundance was going after it . . .

HARSH RECKONING
Phil Ketchum

Five years of keeping himself alive in a brutal prison had made Brand tough and careless about who he gunned down . . .

FARGO: PANAMA GOLD
John Benteen

With foreign money behind him, Buckner was going to destroy the Panama Canal before it could be completed. Fargo's job was to stop Buckner.

FARGO:
THE SHARPSHOOTERS
John Benteen

The Canfield clan, thirty strong were raising hell in Texas. Fargo was tough enough to hold his own against the whole clan.

PISTOL LAW
Paul Evan Lehman

Lance Jones came back to Mustang for just one thing — revenge! Revenge on the people who had him thrown in jail.

HELL RIDERS
Steve Mensing

Wade Walker's kid brother, Duane, was locked up in the Silver City jail facing a rope at dawn. Wade was a ruthless outlaw, but he was smart, and he had vowed to have his brother out of jail before morning!

DESERT OF THE DAMNED
Nelson Nye

The law was after him for the murder of a marshal — a murder he didn't commit. Breen was after him for revenge — and Breen wouldn't stop at anything . . . blackmail, a frameup . . . or murder.

DAY OF THE COMANCHEROS
Steven C. Lawrence

Their very name struck terror into men's hearts — the Comancheros, a savage army of cutthroats who swept across Texas, leaving behind a bloodstained trail of robbery and murder.

SUNDANCE: SILENT ENEMY
John Benteen

A lone crazed Cheyenne was on a personal war path. They needed to pit one man against one crazed Indian. That man was Sundance.

LASSITER
Jack Slade

Lassiter wasn't the kind of man to listen to reason. Cross him once and he'll hold a grudge for years to come — if he let you live that long.

LAST STAGE TO GOMORRAH
Barry Cord

Jeff Carter, tough ex-riverboat gambler, now had himself a horse ranch that kept him free from gunfights and card games. Until Sturvesant of Wells Fargo showed up.

McALLISTER ON THE COMANCHE CROSSING
Matt Chisholm

The Comanche, McAllister owes them a life — and the trail is soaked with the blood of the men who had tried to outrun them before.

QUICK-TRIGGER COUNTRY
Clem Colt

Turkey Red hooked up with Curly Bill Graham's outlaw crew. But wholesale murder was out of Turk's line, so when range war flared he bucked the whole border gang alone . . .

CAMPAIGNING
Jim Miller

Ambushed on the Santa Fe trail, Sean Callahan is saved by two Indian strangers. But there'll be more lead and arrows flying before the band join Kit Carson against the Comanches.

GUNSLINGER'S RANGE
Jackson Cole

Three escaped convicts are out for revenge. They won't rest until they put a bullet through the head of the dirty snake who locked them behind bars.

RUSTLER'S TRAIL
Lee Floren

Jim Carlin knew he would have to stand up and fight because he had staked his claim right in the middle of Big Ike Outland's best grass.

THE TRUTH ABOUT SNAKE RIDGE
Marshall Grover

The troubleshooters came to San Cristobal to help the needy. For Larry and Stretch the turmoil began with a brawl and then an ambush.

WOLF DOG RANGE
Lee Floren

Will Ardery would stop at nothing, unless something stopped him first — like a bullet from Pete Manly's gun.

DEVIL'S DINERO
Marshall Grover

Plagued by remorse, a rich old reprobate hired the Texas Trouble-shooters to deliver a fortune in greenbacks to each of his victims.

GUNS OF FURY
Ernest Haycox

Dane Starr, alias Dan Smith, wanted to close the door on his past and hang up his guns, but people wouldn't let him.

DONOVAN
Elmer Kelton

Donovan was supposed to be dead. Uncle Joe Vickers had fired off both barrels of a shotgun into the vicious outlaw's face as he was escaping from jail. Now Uncle Joe had been shot — in just the same way.

CODE OF THE GUN
Gordon D. Shirreffs

MacLean came riding home, with saddle tramp written all over him, but sewn in his shirt-lining was an Arizona Ranger's star.

GAMBLER'S GUN LUCK
Brett Austen

Gamblers seldom live long. Parker was a hell of a gambler. It was his life — or his death . . .

ORPHAN'S PREFERRED
Jim Miller

Sean Callahan answers the call of the Pony Express and fights Indians and outlaws to get the mail through.

DAY OF THE BUZZARD
T. V. Olsen

All Val Penmark cared about was getting the men who killed his wife.

THE MANHUNTER
Gordon D. Shirreffs

Lee Kershaw knew that every Rurale in the territory was on the lookout for him. But the offer of $5,000 in gold to find five small pieces of leather was too good to turn down.

RIFLES ON THE RANGE
Lee Floren

Doc Mike and the farmer stood there alone between Smith and Watson. There was this moment of stillness, and then the roar would start. And somebody would die . . .

HARTIGAN
Marshall Grover

Hartigan had come to Cornerstone to die. He chose the time and the place, and Main Street became a battlefield.

SUNDANCE: OVERKILL
John Benteen

When a wealthy banker's daughter was kidnapped by the Cheyenne, he offered Sundance $10,000 to rescue the girl.

RIDE A LONE TRAIL
Gordon D. Shirreffs GWJ.

The valley was about to explode into open range war. All it needed was the fuse and Ken Macklin was it.

HARD MAN WITH A GUN
Charles N. Heckelmann

After Bob Keegan lost the girl he loved and the ranch he had sweated blood to build, he had nothing left but his guts and his guns but he figured that was enough.

SUNDANCE: IRON MEN
Peter McCurtin

Sundance, assigned to save the railroad from a murder spree, soon came to realise that he'd have to fight fire with fire, bullets with bullets and death with death!